True Savage 2

Lock Down Publications and Ca$h
Presents
True Savage 2
A Novel by *Chris Green*

True Savage 2

Lock Down Publications
P.O. Box 1482
Pine Lake, Ga 30072-1482

Copyright 2017 by Chris Green True Savage 2

First Edition September 2017
Printed in the United States of America

Lock Down Publications
Like our page on Facebook: Lock Down Publications @
www.facebook.com/lockdownpublications.ldp
Cover design and layout by: **Dynasty Cover Me**
Book interior design by: **Shawn Walker**
Edited by: **Sunny Giovanni**

Stay Connected with Us!

Text **LOCKDOWN** to 22828 to stay up-to-date with new releases, sneak peaks, contests and more...

Thank you!

Submission Guideline.

Submit the first three chapters of your completed manuscript to ldpsubmissions@gmail.com, subject line: Your book's title. The manuscript must be in a .doc file and sent as an attachment. Document should be in Times New Roman, double spaced and in size 12 font. Also, provide your synopsis and full contact information. If sending multiple submissions, they must each be in a separate email.

Have a story but no way to send it electronically? You can still submit to LDP/Ca$h Presents. Send in the first three chapters, written or typed, of your completed manuscript to:

LDP: Submissions Dept
Po Box 1482
Pine Lake, Ga 30072

DO NOT send original manuscript. Must be a duplicate.

Provide your synopsis and a cover letter containing your full contact information.

Thanks for considering LDP and Ca$h Presents.

Chris Green

CHAPTER 1

As D-Lo aimed the gun at Twan's head, two cars pulled up with his two goons rushing out. Twan knew that it was a now or never chance as he jumped off the ground and ran for it. D-Lo quickly fired six shots, trying his best to kill Twan as a bullet struck him in the leg.

Boc! Boc! Boc! Boc! Boc! Boc!

The goons returned fire as the taller bodyguard snatched him off the ground, dragging him inside the car.

As D-Lo and Suave continued to pop their guns, Suave jumped in on the passenger side with D-Lo hopping into the driver's seat before driving off. D-Lo could still hear the bullets ringing out as they flushed away from the daycare towards Oakland City. He made a sharp left on Lorenzo Drive and drove at 100 miles per hour until he reached Avon Street.

"Fuck, fuck, fuck," D-Lo panicked, hitting the dashboard repeatedly. Then, he picked up the phone to call Ghost.

"What happened?" Ghost asked in a calm voice when answering his call.

"I lost that bitch. I shot the fuck out of them, though."

"Fuck. You know what? It's all good. Where is Mariah?"

"She's right here in the backseat. We're on our way over to Tiffany's now."

"Say no more." Ghost quickly hung up.

He automatically knew the situation with Twan was about to get really messy. Tons of blood was already shed from both sides and Ghost was tired of the back and forth. He felt like it was time to really get things heated and search for Twan, live and direct. That day in particular, Ghost knew that he wouldn't stop until Twan was in a box.

D-Lo and Suave pulled into Tiffany's parking lot as Ghost stood outside with his glocc's in hand. After they parked the car, D-Lo grabbed the kid and headed up the walkway. When Ghost saw Mariah he grabbed her and held her as if she was the last living thing on earth. Mariah looked Ghost in the eyes as she held on to his neck tightly.

"Tiffany," Ghost yelled as they all walked inside the house.

Tiffany hurried to Ghost's call. "Yes, baby?"

"Get all of our shit packed up. We're leaving." Ghost moved quickly as he sat Mariah down on the couch.

"I'm on it right now," she yelled, heading to the back of the apartment.

"D-Lo, call up the team and let them know everything stops today. No more movement, period. Let them know we're relocating the Mobb, ASAP."

"I got ya', lil' bro." D-Lo jumped on the line to put things into motion.

Ghost retrieved his phone out of his pocket and dialed Shadow's number. The phone rang twice into Ghost's ear before he picked up.

"What's good, folk?"

"What's good, bro? I need you, ASAP. We're ending this shit today," he whispered, looking over at Tre's daughter on the couch.

"I'm on my way," Shadow said in a hurry, just before he hung up the phone.

"Whoa, Tiff!" Ghost yelled.

She walked back into the living room. "Yes, daddy?"

"Call the moving company and let them know we will pay whatever expense we got to for a full move out of the state. We're leaving Atlanta tonight."

"Okay, baby." She then rushed to get on the phone to make it happen. "Where do I tell them we're going?"

Ghost thought for a minute as he looked up at the ceiling and back at her. "Tell 'em we're going to California," he responded, patting Mariah's back.

Tiffany shook her head as she placed the call to the moving company.

When the team started to arrive, Ghost walked down into the basement to prepare for the final standoff with Twan.

It didn't matter if he had to stay out all night until they found him, he was ending the confusion that day. And the only way he felt it would end was a bullet between the eyes.

When the team saw Ghost reappear upstairs in his gear, they knew it was officially time to get on the bullshit. D-Lo, Tim, J.L., Hotboy and Chucc were posted in the living room as four other goons stood outside.

"Tim, J.L., I need y'all to go and pick up Erica. Bring her over here. I don't care what she has to say, make her ass come."

"Say no more, Don," Tim said. He and J.L. left the house.

Ghost walked over to D-Lo, then whispered in his ear. "You know where the stash is. Grab everything— guns and all. No one is to see that, not even Erica."

"You know I'ma handle it," he mouthed. He walked out of the house and got in his car to follow Tim and J.L.

When Shadow finally arrived, Ghost grabbed his guns and slid them inside his waistband. Then, he walked over to Tiffany, kissed her on the forehead and headed towards the door. As he got to the entrance, he looked over at Suave. "I want you to hold the post and make sure everything is all the way good."

Suave assured him with a serious head nod as Ghost walked out of the house.

While Suave sat in the living room with Chucc and Tiffany, he watched Chucc as he eyed her with a sexual look and disrespectful gestures. He made it his business to keep a close eye out for this nigga instead of telling Ghost. It was something Suave wasn't sure about when he looked at Chucc.

Ever since he's been here, he's been eyeing sis with that nasty ass smile, Suave thought.

He told Chucc to step out on the porch so Tiffany could have some privacy and finish getting their things packed. Chucc wanted to say something slick until he saw how hard Suave was clutching the F and N in his hand.

"Yeah, a'ite homie," Chucc said, walking towards the door.

Riding in the car quietly, Shadow and Ghost cruised to Twan's neck of the woods. They were eyeing everyone who looked like they were a part of his team. Shadow slowed the car down as he pointed at Twan coming out of the rundown trap spot. Ghost grabbed the AR-15 from the backseat as Shadow held on to his two fifty round clip Macs.

Twan had four goons surrounding him as they all walked to the car. Shadow looked at Ghost, giving him a nod that said he was ready. They both jumped out of the car with no talking, letting their guns bark.

Boc! Boc! Boc! Boc! Boc! Boc! Boc!

Twan's goons immediately started to return fire after Ghost killed one of his men instantly. Cars in traffic hurried about as the commotion became intense.

Twan took off running through the pathway on the side of the house as Shadow squeezed his triggers, ripping down everything in Twan's path. Ghost shot it out boldly. With the two bodyguards, Shadow proceeded to chase after Twan. Seeing Shadow gaining on him, when looking back, Twan released his gun over his shoulder. Heart pounded with fear. Shadow ducked and maneuvered through the woods while releasing his Mac Two, putting gigantic holes in the tree inches from Twan's head.

Twan's adrenaline was pumping harder than ever as he pulled the trigger on his gun and nothing came out. "Fuck," he said as he dropped the pistol on the ground and continued to run.

Twan exited from the pathway but his face was met with the handle of Ghost's AR-15, splitting his lip in two.

"You can't outrun this Challenger, bitch," Ghost yelled as he put the gun towards Twan's face.

Shadow made his way out of the cut, seeing Ghost standing over Twan. As he had gotten closer, he asked, "What happened to the other two bodyguards?"

"They all having a little meeting with God right now. We got one more first class trip."

As Twan spit a heap of blood out his mouth and looked up at Ghost, he smiled awkwardly. "You can't run, nigga. My family's coming for you, and they ain't gone stop until you and all your family's gone, fuck boy!" He shouted, feeling that this was the end.

"Oh yeah. And I'ma make sure I splat all their asses, just like I did you."

"Fuck you, pussy," Twan grunted as they all heard the police sirens from a distance.

Ghost smirked as he put the choppa to his face. "Say cheese, fuck nigga."

The AR ripped apart Twan's face as it popped loudly. *Poc! Poc! Poc! Poc! Poc! Poc! Poc! Poc! Poc!*

Ghost shot Twan nine times and watched as his body inhaled its last breath. Afterward, Ghost and Shadow ran to the car and jumped in. They flushed 85 miles per hour towards Campbellton and Delowe Drive. Ghost made a left through the Marathon gas station and drove under the bridge until he reached the express way.

"So, what now?" Shadow asked, looking over at Ghost.

"Same thing. We finna get the fuck out the A, get money, and if a fuck nigga get in our way in Cali, they gone feel the pain and drop tears as well."

Shadow slid on his Ray Bands as he sat back in his seat. "Let's do it then."

CHAPTER 2

Money, Pain & Tears
6 Months later in Beverly Hills, CA

Ghost pulled up to his five-bedroom, two story home. He parked his car next to Shadow's as he grabbed his cell phone and got out. D-Lo sat outside in his new S.S. Camaro, blowing a blunt of Moon Rock as he listened to his iPad. Ghost dapped up his brother and continued into the house.

Walking into the massive crib, Shadow was stretched out on the couch. Ghost walked by, kicking the couch, making him jump out of his sleep.

"Ghost, you're gonna make me slice your goddamn balls off, messing with me while I'm sleep, motherfucker," Shadow said, wiping his eyes.

Ghost laughed and flicked a bird as he kept moving up the steps. Walking into the bedroom, Tiffany sat in the mirror, hot-combing her hair while Laylah laid on the bed, chewing on the remote. Ghost picked his one month old daughter up, pulling the controller away from her.

"Why you thewing on dat wemote," Ghost asked in a playish voice.

Laylah laughed as she grabbed Ghost's face, chewing on his lip.

"Daddy's baby looks just like him." He laughed, kissing his daughter before laying her back down.

He walked over to Tiffany in the mirror, then hugged her Coke bottle frame.

Ever since Tiffany had Layla, she had gotten even badder. Her ass was twice as fatter than before. Her hair grew twice the length it used to be. And her breast were more round, making her body more of the video vixen type. Ghost sucked on Tiffany's neck as she tried to balance the curling irons in her hand.

"Mmm shit," she moaned. Then, she turned around, jumping up in his arms. "And where have you been all morning, mister? Your daughter acts as if you're leaving earth forever."

"Oh yeah?" He mouthed, kissing Tiffany's lips.

"Yes. I don't know how she's so smart at a month and a half. She's fucking spoiled Ghost."

"I know that." Ghost began stripping off his clothes, looking at her seductively before heading to the shower.

Tiffany looked at him with a wide smile. She followed him in, closing the door behind her.

"You betta watch my child while she on that bed," Ghost smirked at her behind him as he was turning on the shower.

"I just want to get some of my man before you take it to that ungrateful bitch across town."

Ghost laughed as Tiffany released him out of his boxers and licked all over his private. After sucking his skin off for five minutes straight, she pulled down her shorts and let Ghost take her from the back. Ghost pumped a little forceful after he entered Tiffany's wet pussy. Ever since she dropped Laylah, her pussy was 10 times better. He slapped Tiffany's ass as she moaned and threw it back for him to fuck her harder. Tiffany was so wet that Ghost slipped out of her twice and reentered her sweet cookie.

"Damn, daddy!"

As he kept his pace, watching her butt move back and forth, he exploded inside of her, enjoying the euphoria. Tiffany threw her ass back a couple more times and slid off of his rod. She jumped in the shower for fifteen minutes. After she bathed, she put on her clothes, leaving him behind in the shower.

After Ghost finished showering, he put on his clothes, came out the bathroom and headed downstairs. Tiffany laid on the couch watching Frozen with Laylah on the 60-inch plasma TV. He kissed her head and did the same to Laylah as he headed out the door. Shadow sat on the front porch talking to D-Lo.

"Whoa, I'll be back," Ghost said, walking down the steps.

"Ghost, wait a minute. I need to holla at you, bro." Shadow said with all seriousness.

"Hold off until I get back. I gotta go pick the baby up from Erica."

"Ghost this is important."

"Well it will still be important when I get back, nigga. It won't take more than thirty minutes."

Hopping inside the Porsche truck, he started the foreign and pulled off.

Ghost rode through the streets of Beverly Hills, bumping his music as he observed and took in the scenery. Leaving Atlanta six months ago was the best thing Ghost felt he had done. Even though Erica and Tiffany didn't get along, they both respected that he had children to raise and his mind frame of everyone being a family. Erica disagreed to move in a house with Tiffany and share her man with another woman. When Ghost broke the news to her four months ago that Tiffany was pregnant, Erica slapped him in the face and didn't answer his phone calls for three weeks straight. After he forcefully went and made love to her for three hours, she forgave him but couldn't get over the fact that Tiffany was having his child.

Ghost pulled up to the four-bedroom, two-story home and cut his car off. He jumped out, heading to the door. He inserted his key and went inside. Seeing that the living room was empty, he walked upstairs where Erica laid on her side, playing with Bernard. Ghost took off his shoes and climbed in the bed with his son. Bernard looked at Ghost, smiling when seeing his father's face. He squealed with laughter as Ghost blew on his stomach.

Erica smiled as she looked at the two most important people in her life. She knew that her and Ghost went through their ugly situations but he always took care of home.

"And how have you been, Ms. Lady?" Ghost asked, leaning over his little one to plant kisses gently on her lips.

"I'm good, daddy. Are we still on for our family picnic tomorrow, or do you have other plans?"

"Of course, and as soon as you and Tiffany stop the bullshit y'all doing, we can all be a family."

Erica smacked her teeth loudly from his remark. "Ghost, how can you get two females pregnant and think that we all supposed to be a jolly, happy family? Where is the joy in sharing my man with another woman?"

"First of all, shit ain't all about you. You're right, you shouldn't have to share your man at all, but I messed up. Nobody's perfect. But realize it or not, we're all family. So, instead of hating each other and always finding something to argue about, we should be loving each other and leaving our differences on the sideline. Don't I take care of you and my son?"

"Yeah."

"Don't I make love to you and give Tiffany the same treatment?"

"I guess," she answered, disliking the remark.

"No, you know, because if I didn't, I wouldn't be here right now. I love you, Erica. No one can stop me from being with you and my son. Pull your head out ya' ass and stop being so jealous." Ghost pecked her lips and picked Bernard up to go and watch some Saturday cartoons.

Erica sat on the bed thinking about what Ghost said. Her phone rung. When she saw the private number, she stepped into the bathroom and closed the door. "Hello?"

"Agent Harper, this is Director Farmer. I'm calling you in regard to your case."

"Uh, yes, sir?"

"Agent Harper, you've been with our suspect and still haven't gained any new evidence on him. He's under FBI investigation, and from where we stand, it looks like you're trying to build a family. Tell us where you are and we will send an emergency team in to get you."

"I'm sorry sir, I can't do that just yet." Erica knew in her heart that if she traded on Ghost right now, he really might kill her.

"Agent Harper, if you violate protocol for this mission, you will be placed into Federal custody." Director Farmer said coldly.

"Just give me a little time and I'll get him to come in," Erica begged.

"I'm sorry, Agent Harper, at this time you've been taken off the case. Either tell us where you are and turn him in for questioning, or there will be Federal warrants out for you both."

"Well I'm afraid that's just what it's gonna have to be, sir." She looked down, hanging up the line.

Erica thought about going in the living room to tell Ghost everything, but she didn't want him to feel betrayed.

She felt the terrible burden on her heart and promised herself she would tell Ghost everything before it was too late.

As Erica opened the bathroom door, Ghost stood on the other side, making her jump.

"Who you talking to?" Ghost asked, looking at Erica like she was crazy.

"Nobody, baby. What are you talking about?" She swiftly moved pass him, fidgeting, thinking Ghost might have over heard her conversation.

"Hmm, I thought I heard you talking to somebody. What time are you leaving to go shopping?"

"In about twenty minutes. I don't want to be out long."

Ghost shook his head. "Well I'm taking Bernard with me over to the other house while you're gone, to at least try and let his sisters be with him for a while."

She nodded her head as Ghost sat down, playfully tickling Bernard.

"Okay baby."

Ghost felt the vibe as he looked at her with a strange eye. "Are you sure you're okay?"

"Of course, baby. Why wouldn't I be?" Erica said, flashing a fake smile.

"Okay."

After grabbing his things, he walked off to get Bernard ready. Once his son was beyond spiffy, Ghost left out of the house to the car. Strapping his son in the car seat, he checked both of his shoulder holsters and hopped into the driver's seat. Ghost rode until he reached the other side of town in Los Angeles. When he arrived at his destination, he made a right on E. 137th Street and parked the whip.

Getting out of the car, Ghost grabbed Bernard and walked on the porch, knocking on the burglar bar door.

"Who is it?" The voice said from the other side of the door.

"It's me," Ghost replied.

Unlatching the locks, J.L. opened the door, letting Ghost in.

"Wassup, dawg?" J.L. asked giving Ghost some dap.

"And wassup with my nephew?" J.L. grabbed Bernard and continued to walk deeper into the house.

Three women sat in the kitchen bagging up dope while Suave and Tim sat in the corner counting money.

"Wat up my brother?" Tim asked.

"Nun much, y'all nigga's good?"

"As always," they responded in unison.

"What the count looking like right now?"

"Right now, it's six hundred eighty-three thousand, but looking at how much we gotta go, it's probably about seven-o-five or seven-o-one," Suave replied, thumbing through the bills with expertise.

"This shit starting to get real low, Don. We probably working with like ten of them thangs. Besides that, ain't nothing left but some weed," Tim voiced.

"I know, we gotta find a new fucking plug, man. This shit ain't like Atlanta. Everybody's all tight and scared around this motherfucker."

"Don't worry, I think it's 'bout time to start moving some of that real city muscle out here," Tim suggested with a smile.

"Now that's what the fuck I'm saying," Suave agreed. He raised his gun in the air, pretending he was blowing someone's head off.

"Y'all niggas take a break from this shit. Bring the bitches with ya'. Let's hit the crib and kick shit for a minute. I gotta go check out that open space for that strip joint I'm trying to open up."

Pulling out his iPhone, Ghost started to type something into the keypad.

"Fucking right, we don't need nothing but some bad bitch's in there," Tim said as they all gathered up the money and drugs.

As everybody left the trap for that day, they got in the whips and headed across town to Ghost's house.

Pulling into the driveway two cars deep, Shadow, D-Lo, and Tiffany stood on the porch as Ghost and the team stepped out of the cars and headed for the door.

"Daddy!" Mariah screamed as she ran and jumped in Ghost's arm.

"Hey, Daddy baby, where have you been all day?" Ghost asked.

"I was sleeping, daddy, and you were gone when I woke up," Mariah said, looking into his eyes.

"Aww, it's okay baby. Daddy's back."

Even though Mariah wasn't Ghost's biological child he catered to her as one of his own for the strength of Tre. After Ghost sat Mariah down she ran into her uncle Suave's arms and held him tightly. When Ghost looked up he saw the stale faces of D-Lo, Shadow and Tiffany.

Ghost made his way to the porch as he eyed his brother. "What's going on?"

"Look, Ghost," Shadow said, speaking first. "It's something going on with Erica."

"What the fuck you mean something going on with her? I just left her." Ghost replied aggressively.

"Calm down, Ghost, I've been following her for the past few days and she's not right, bro." Shadow vouched, handing Ghost the pictures that was in his hand.

When Ghost saw the photos of her in an FBI jacket, holding a gun, his heart instantly sank.

"She's a fucking Fed, bro." Shadow looked on with an angry expression.

Ghost continued to flip through the photos as the grey sky started drizzling rain. Shadow could see the worry on his face as he held the photos

"Her parents have been dead since 2008. They died in a car crash on 285th. A year and a half later she graduated from Harvard University in Criminal Justice and Psychology. She's setting you up, bro."

Ghost's heart was so blank. He remembered when he found the handgun in her nightstand six months ago. He always wondered about her suspicious disappearing acts when she claimed she was pulling a double at work. Ghost's heart turned cold and black as he bald up the pictures. Everyone stood around as they looked at him for the next move.

"Do you want me to handle it, bruh?" D-Lo asked, feeling the pain floating off his brother.

"Naw, I'ma kill this bitch on my own. Tiff, you and D-Lo go and check out that space tonight for the club. If it's nice, buy it and tell them if they start working right away we will pay extra."

"I got you, daddy." Tiffany said, kissing Ghost.

"Are you sure you don't want anyone to come with you?" Shadow asked, looking concerned.

"I got it," was all that he got out before walking off the porch in the rain.

Getting back inside his whip, he crank up his car and smashed off as he thought about how many ways he could kill Erica. After everything he'd been through with running from the Feds he had one right under his nose. Ghost always saw the signs and still couldn't put his finger on it, but today it would end.

As Ghost arrived back at the other house, he washed his hands and began to prepare Erica's dinner.

He pulled out all the ingredients he would need to make the French Gumbo. Once he had gotten everything into a single pot, he turned the eye on the stove down to let the food simmer and cook. When the pot started to boil, Ghost added three small cups of rat poisoning and stirred it in a slow motion.

He carefully put the lid on the pot and walked back towards the bathroom. He began to run the water for her bath as he added a light squeeze of bubble works. When he finished running the water, he opened the bottle of chloroform and poured in two full caps. Closing the top on it, he stashed it under the bathroom cabinet and went back to the kitchen. He looked at his watch and sat at the table until Erica arrived.

Thirty minutes later, Erica walked in with tons of shopping bags across her arms. She sat her things down in the living room when seeing Ghost sitting at the table.

"Hey, baby," Erica said, pecking his lips.

Ghost barely returned her kiss as she raised up looking him in the eyes.

"Are you okay?" She asked, feeling the bad vibe coming from him.

"I'm good, ma," Ghost flashed a fake smile. "I made lunch for you. Sit down," he ordered, getting up to retrieve her a plate.

Erica sat at the table as the strange feeling began rumbling in her stomach. After Ghost sat the plate in front of her, she instantly felt her belly turn. "Baby, I'm actually not that hungry."

"You haven't even tried it yet," Ghost said with a stale look on his face.

"I just had some pizza earlier that messed my stomach up real bad. I just want to take a bath and lay down."

"Okay." Ghost walked over, picked her plate up and scraped it back inside the pot.

"Ghost?"

"Yes?"

"Where is Bernard?"

"I asked D-Lo to watch him so we can get some alone time." He could smell the fear on her skin as he turned back around to continue what he was doing.

As Erica walked in the room, she grabbed her towel and eased in the bathroom. She locked the door as she pulled her 380 pistol from her ankle holster. Undressing, she sat her gun under her clothes on the toilet and slowly stepped into the water. After two minutes in the tub, Erica became drowsy. She laid her head back against the barrier of the tub. After a few minutes, she thought that she saw the door knob wiggle hard before it came crashing in.

Ghost ran over to Erica, pointing his gun at her head.

"Baby, what's wrong?" She asked terrified.

Ghost shot her twice in the head making her body sink into the tub.

Erica gasped for air as she woke out of her horrific dream. Her fingers and her body were wrinkled from sitting in the water so long. Realizing that she had fallen asleep, Erica tried to stand and almost fell out of the tub. She wondered what the hell was wrong with her body as she held on to the wall, feeling herself about to tilt. Her legs were as soft as Jell-O and she couldn't hold her balance. She unlocked the bathroom door and stepped on the hardwood floor. She took one step and almost slipped on the baby oil that was squirted across the ground.

She looked up to see Ghost cocking his gun and aiming it at her.

"If you move I'll blow a hole directly through yo' brain."

"Ghost, why are you pointing that gun at me?" Erica mumbled trying to balance herself as her heartbeat sped up.

"Where are your parents, Erica?"

"I told you my parents stay in New York, Chance," Erica replied with a sad expression.

"I found your parents' death certificates in your shit. They were signed by you in 2008." Ghost threw the crumbled up pictures that Shadow gave him at her feet. "What the fuck are those?" He asked with anger.

Erica looked at the pictures and back up at Ghost as she started to drop tears. "I promise I was going to tell you, Ghost."

"When? After y'all built a case on me?" Ghost screamed.

"Baby, you have to believe me."

Ghost got up off the bed and walked over to Erica, punching her in the face. She crumbled to the floor as Ghost grabbed her hair, dragging her to the bathroom. She screamed, begging him to stop, but her body was so weak she couldn't even fight back. Ghost snatched her by the tub as he dunked her head inside of the water. Erica's naked body kicked across the floor as he held her head. Pulling her up, Erica chocked harshly as he held her neck.

"So how long you been plotting on taking me down, bitch?" He fumed as he slammed her head back into the water. He raised her back up and punched her with a left hand, causing her to fall into the wall. Ghost bent down beside her as he put his pistol inside of her mouth. "Give me one reason why I shouldn't blow your brains all over the floor!" He yelled, looking on as she laid against the wall helplessly.

Her face began to swell quickly as she tried to catch her breath. "Ghost, I love you, I will never turn on you for anyone."

Ghost pushed the gun inside her mouth harder. "Try again, dumb bitch."

Tears began to flush down her face as she looked up into his eyes. "Because I had your son. I promise I was gonna tell you, Ghost. I was scared that this would happen. You and my son are all I have. Don't leave me, Chance."

"You lucky you my kid's mom, bitch. You got two days to leave California or the next time I see your face, I'll make sure to put two bullets in it. And just so you know, you ain't ever seeing my kid again." Ghost said, walking out of the bathroom leaving her to die.

Chris Green

CHAPTER 3

Ghost cruised in his whip as he thought about what he did to Erica. She betrayed all the trust that they worked so hard to build. He thought about going back and blowing her brains out as he drove through the city, trying to clear his mind. He couldn't help but keep looking in the rearview mirror expecting the cops to jump on him.

He pulled into a nearby strip and bar joint that he spotted to clear his mind. Walking in he bought him a drink of Hennessy after he sat at the bar. The strip club was halfway empty with three women on stage dancing slowly to the music that was playing in the background. Ghost chugged down his drink as a thick chocolate woman crawled towards him. He watched as the woman pulled out her breast and started to lick her nipple.

Ghost pulled off $300 and slid the bills into the girl's panty line.

"Is that all I can do for you, daddy?" The girl asked, flashing a peek of her pink kitten.

His dick instantly became hard as she spread her pussy lips.

Ghost started rubbing his finger across her clit as she looked in his face. "What will it cost me?"

The stripper hopped off of stage, grabbed his hand and led him through the back. Walking into the private room, rose pedals sat on the floor around a soft, red couch as Miguel played softly on the speakers.

The stripper slid her thong off and spread her ass cheeks, showing Ghost her sweetness. He sat comfortably on the couch while she gave him a lap dance to the song that filled the air. The girl turned around, unzipping

Ghost's pants to let him hang out. Using no hands, the stripper used her tongue lifting Ghost into her mouth to suck on him slowly. The stripper used two hands as she bobbed her head up and down on his length. Ghost grabbed the back of her head as she licked his baseline and put his balls into her mouth. She let him choke her as she tried to eat everything he had to offer. The stripper stood up over him and pulled the magnum condom out of her bra.

After she placed the rubber on Ghost, she turned around, squatting on top of him as he grabbed her ass. The girl rode Ghost, taking all of him as she moaned to the top of her lungs. She reached under him, playing with his balls as he plunged inside of her.

"Aww, right there, baby," she said as Ghost held her leg, making sure she stayed in place.

Ghost rubbed her pussy as he stroked smoothly, making her climax on top of him, while keeping her pace. The woman raised one leg on the couch, turning to the side when riding Ghost so she could see his face. He looked into her eyes, slapping her ass as she rode harder. After fifteen minutes Ghost released himself-inside of the rubber, as the girl laid back on his chest.

He palmed the stripper's ass slowly as he looked at her. "So how much do I owe you?"

"How good yo' dick is, daddy you can hit this pussy for free when you want."

"Oh yeah?" He asked, looking into her eyes. "What's your name, ma?"

"Tweety," she replied, raising up to snap her bra back on.

"Tweety, huh?" Ghost grabbed the pen that was sitting on the little glass table and wrote his number on a $100 bill.

Handing her the money, he smiled at her kinkiness. "When you bored, or need some, don't hesitate."

Tweety took the bill and put it in her bra. Leaning down, she sucked on Ghost's bottom lip as they shared a kiss. "Bye, big daddy," she said, getting up to walk out of the room.

After Ghost headed to the bathroom and cleaned up, he left out, jumping back into his Porsche Truck. As he headed back towards the other side of town, Ghost's phone rang. Seeing Dillon's name flash across the screen, he picked up. "Whoa, what's good, bro?" Ghost answered, keeping his eye on the road.

"Shit, nun much, my boy. I'm just checking in with ya', letting you know everything running smooth in the A right now. We laid back and shit really been easy, ever since ho-mie been in God's Land." Dillon said laughing.

Ghost chuckled at his remark.

"So, how have things been in Bel-Air?"

"It's alright, but weird as fuck. People are wondering how a whole bunch of ghetto motherfuckers can afford a two-million-dollar crib and nobody works."

"Welcome to the dope game, bitch," Dillion laughed. "But the money is being expressed your way as we speak."

"Understood." Ghost ended the call and continued over to his spot.

Pulling into his spot, Ghost jumped out of his whip and headed into the house.

D-Lo sat on the couch, talking to his girl on the phone as he walked in. "Let me call you back," D-Lo said, hanging up his cell. He looked at Ghost as he sat on the couch and leaned his head back. "You couldn't do it, could you?"

Ghost fired up his blunt and took a deep breath. "Naw, I couldn't. But I damn sho tried to."

"Was she breathing when you left?"

"Yeah, but she looked like she was finna die from lack of oxygen." Ghost laughed, smiling crazily.

D-Lo shook his head as he thought about how much harm she actually could be to their entire operation. "Do you think she gonna tell?"

Ghost shook his head dismissively. "That bitch ain't gone tell, I gave her ass two days to get out of Cali. If she ain't gone by then, I'ma dump the bitch in a bucket of acid."

D-Lo just chuckled as he accepted the Garcia Vega from his brother's hand.

"How did that spot look today?" Ghost asked, changing the subject.

"Nigga, that shit was dumb fye. They down there working on it as we speak. How much bread Tiffany skinned down, they said they will be done with it by the end of next week."

"That's my bitch." Ghost smiled, shaking his head in approval. "You know what, call everybody up and tell them we throwing a party at the house tonight. I need to celebrate for the opening of this club."

D-Lo coughed from the blunt as he walked through the hallway to the bedroom. "Say no mo."

Before you know it, the hours passed along and the whole team was jam-packed inside of the house. Ghost invited the neighbors so he wouldn't have to hear their mouths the next morning. Chucc and Hotboy showed up with a bitch parade and a bag full of addictions as the party started to fill in.

Tiffany walked around the living room passing out Patron and Ciroc Jell-O shots to the crowd. The party was extra live as everybody started passing the weed around. The house got so packed that Ghost had to open the patio to the pool deck.

D-Lo crank the action up as he dove from the second floor, hitting a gainer inside the massive pool. The radio bumped T.I.'s song *Hell of a Life* through the speakers which made all the females jump in the pool.

Ghost sat on the side of the pool, smoking his white owl blunt as Tiffany brought the kids out to the water. He looked at her two-piece sinking between her butt cheeks. Moving quickly, he licked his lips and got up from where he was sitting. Ghost grabbed a handful of Tiffany's ass as she rocked to the music.

"Why you out here showing all daddy goodies," he asked, licking Tiffany on her back.

Tiffany closed her eyes and licked her lips as she turned to Ghost. "If you don't want me to take these two pieces off and jump on that dick in front of everybody, you betta stop."

"Alright, when everybody goes to sleep, you know what time it is," Ghost teased, giving her a freaky smile.

Tiffany pouted. "Ouhh, baby, is it gonna hurt?" She smiled, giving Ghost her green puppy dog eyes.

"You'll see." Ghost winked as he walked off.

The party stayed amped until one in the morning and the neighbors nearby threatened to call the police. Everyone was so high and wasted off liquor that over thirty people were passed out on Ghost's living room floor. Ghost laughed, stepping over all the bodies in the living room as he went to check on his kids. After he saw that everybody was okay, he kept his promise and headed in the room with Tiffany.

Ghost held Tiffany's arm behind her as he dug in from the back. Her ass clapped loudly against his body and the love making could be clearly heard from the hallway. He stood up, placing his back against the wall as he lifted her up. Holding her ass, he grind inside of her as she rotated her hips. Tiffany held on to Ghost's neck as she released herself on his lovesick.

Her cum trickled down his stomach as he continued to penetrate her. Ghost laid her down gently on the bed as he buried his face in between her legs. After he felt her satisfaction was complete, he took her to the bathroom where they bathed in a long, hot shower and passed out minutes later, cuddling in the bed.

The next morning, Ghost was woken from the loud banging that erupted on his front door. He jumped out of bed grabbing his gun as he slid on his pants. Everybody else in the house was fully awake as the action started to begin.

"Bitch, what is your fucking problem? Do you got a death wish or something?" Ghost asked Erica after they all stepped on the front porch.

Erica's face was running with tears. Her left eye was black and her right jaw was slightly swollen. "Ghost, baby, I need to talk to you," Erica begged, looking at him sincerely.

"You need to raise the fuck up outta here," Tim demanded, clutching his pistol, waiting for Ghost's command.

"Tim, you have nothing to do with me and my child's father. Stay out of this. Chance, I'm not leaving until you talk to me."

The words she spoke landed on deaf ears as he looked in her eyes like she was pathetic. "Tim, show this silly ass girl where her car is." Ghost shrugged, getting bored with the situation instantly.

As Tim tried to grab Erica, she chopped him in the throat and took his pistol away, putting it up to Ghost's temple. D-Lo tried to pull out his burner but was a second too late. Erica pulled her spare, pressing the 380 automatic against his chest.

"Baby!" Erica screamed, crying harder. "I will kill you before you just walk away from me."

"Put the gun down." He whispered calmly.

"D-Lo, I love you like a brother, but I'm warning you, don't do it," Erica raged, pressing her gun in his chest harder.

D-Lo's face stiffened as he eased his hand back down at his side.

"I'm gonna tell you one more time, Erica. Take this gun away from my head. You have a lot on your plate, and before you do something you're gonna highly regret, I suggest you calm down." He pleaded, feeling the steel on his head.

Tiffany stepped from behind Ghost and put her baby glocc 23 in Erica's face.

"Tiffany, you have nothing to do with this," Erica glanced quickly, trying to keep her eyes on Ghost.

"I do when you got a gun to my brother and my nigga's head."

"He's my man bitch!" Erica shouted, shifting both of the guns on Tiffany in a second.

"How can he be your man when you lied to him about being a fucking pig?"

"Fuck you, I did it to protect him. If I was so much of an FBI bitch he would have been locked up months ago."

"You know what? Fuck all this small talk. Show me what you really talking about," she spat, passing her gun to D-Lo.

"Bitch, you ain't said nothing." Erica looked at her with a funny expression, giving her guns to Ghost. "Come on, hoe."

Tiffany rushed Erica, catching her violently on the right cheek. She stumbled slightly. Regaining her balance, she punched Tiffany in her side and kneed her in the stomach. As they tumbled and held each other, she scooped Erica off the ground, slamming her against her back and followed up with a three piece. Erica grabbed Tiffany's hair, head butting her and pushed her over. As she got up, standing over her Erica, wasted no time kicking her in the stomach.

"Get up, bitch!" She screamed.

Tiffany scurried to her feet, shaking the kick off. Once she regained her composure the girls went blow for blow until Ghost felt like it was enough.

He stepped in, grabbing Tiffany as D-Lo held Erica.

"Let me go, I'm gonna rip her fucking head off," Erica exploded, kicking and screaming like a mad woman.

"Shut the fuck up, bitch, you ain't gone do squat," Tiffany said calm as if nothing ever happened.

Ghost grabbed Tiffany's face gently and looked at her. The right upper part of her eye, just above her lash, was swollen. Her lip was slightly busted as the small line of blood dripped down to her shirt. "Good shit ma, go clean up," he whispered, patting her on the butt.

"Okay, daddy," she replied, walking off into the house.

Tim and the team stood to the sideline as they watched the chaos unfold. Ghost walked over to Erica as she stood in the grass by the sidewalk. Her nose was busted and her jaw was swelling horribly. When he stood in front of her, she sat with her arms folded and started crying.

"Baby, I'm sorry. Please don't leave me, Chance! You and my son are the best thing that has ever happened to me. Don't just walk away," she pleaded, looking exhausted.

He almost wanted to shed a tear seeing Erica in the position she was in. She even fought with Tiffany to prove a point about her love. Not only that, she put a gun to his head.

"Look at me," Ghost said, making her jump. "I love you but you lost my trust, you lost my respect. Honesty is key to any relationship and you broke that key. So, you gotta earn my trust back, understand?"

Erica shook her head as she began to spill her tears harder.

"What about your job?" Ghost asked.

"They told me if I don't turn you in within the next ten days, or tell them where we are, they're going to put out a warrant for my arrest."

"So, what you gonna do?"

Erica looked at him awkwardly as if he just insulted her. "I'm gonna ride with you until both of us is in a casket, six feet under," she spoke as she walked off.

In the back of Ghost's head was a huge smile, knowing he had Erica where he wanted her. He watched as she got in her car and pulled off. Now was the time to officially put his plan in effect.

As Erica drove home and thought about her sticky situation, she prayed to herself that she could get her family back. After she got home, she got in the shower and let the hot steam wash away her pain. She stayed in the water and soaked for twenty minutes until she was numbed. Finishing her shower, she took three Tylenol and climbed in the bed, looking at the picture of her, Ghost and Bernard. The tears started to pour again as she balled up in her covers, crying herself to sleep.

It was late into the night when she was woken from the wet, soft licks of Ghost's tongue. Erica moved the covers to watch him lick her clit back and forth.

"Ohh, babyy, I'm sorry." She trembled and arched her back from Ghost's lips.

"It's okay, baby," he spoke, missing her sweet taste. He nibbled on her clit softly as he stuck his hand inside of her oven to tickle her G-spot. He put hickies on her legs, then stood up to drop his boxers. "You gone tell me how sorry you are?" he asked her as he flipped her over on her knees."

"I'm sorry, daddy," she moaned as if she were about receive a beating.

Ghost climbed on the bed and entered Erica from the back. He held her shoulders, coming out as far as he could, and reentered her over and over as she let him take her to an amazing ecstasy. He slapped her ass roughly, making her arch her back a little more. Ghost pulled out before he came and flipped Erica on her back. He dove into her as she crossed her legs around his back. She sucked greedily on Ghost's neck as he licked between her breast to make her cum. He took his time for the rest of the night and had his way with her until she fell into a deep sleep on his chest.

CHAPTER 4

The next day crept upon them quickly as the sun lifted brightly above the horizon. Erica was awakened by the smell that invaded her nose. She knew that it was Ghost cooking. It reminded her of when they first met. As she walked into the kitchen, Ghost didn't say a word to her. He sat the plate at the table in front of her and sat opposite in the chair across from her.

"I'm sorry, daddy," Erica mumbled softly, looking across the table at Ghost.

He put his finger to his lips, quieting her. "I know you are," he said, leaning across the table to give her a passionate kiss. "I'll be back later on. You need to go by the house and spend some time with Bernard."

Erica shook her head as Ghost looked into her eyes.

"No fighting with Tiffany either, or I'ma whip both of y'all asses."

"Okay." Erica replied as she looked at him.

Placing her hand on her chest, she thanked God that he still had an ounce of love for her somewhere. She knew in the back of her head eventually things would begin to get shaky. After closing her eyes and saying a silent prayer, she began finishing her breakfast.

Ghost cruised through Beverly Hills and even Culver City to find some of the best designer clothes he could. His club was opening in another week, and being the boss means you had to look like the boss. Today, Ghost was holding auditions for dancers at his club. No matter how bad you were, you had to be screened for a disease test. Under no circumstances was a girl allowed to sell her body, and Tiffany would be the one to decide whether the girl gets the job or not, and of course, she had to have the looks, body and dance skills.

After Ghost finished shopping, he pulled into the main entrance of Fed Ex and parked his car. Walking into the building, Ghost gave the lady his fake name, ID and 3 men came from the back with a box a piece. The men helped Ghost carry the boxes to the car and he tipped them a $100 apiece. Ghost got in his car, swerving off as he called D-Lo.

"Whoa," D-Lo said, sounding half way sleep.

"Come outside in like 20 minutes and help me with these boxes."

"Say less."

Hanging up the phone, Ghost rode patiently to the house as he thought to himself. Things was starting to get confusing. A lot of pieces were placed in his life that he couldn't understand.

As he pulled into the drive way, D-Lo came out and helped him load the boxes inside the living room. Erica sat on the floor with Bernard in her hand while Tiffany came down the steps.

"What's this, daddy," she questioned, kissing Ghost on the cheek.

"Monthly count from Dillon."

Erica sat and watched as Ghost burst the boxes open. Blocks and bundles of money fell on the floor when Ghost cut through the plastic that held the paper together. D-Lo and Ghost began to flip through the paper as Erica stared in amazement of how much money she was really seeing. Tiffany joined in and it was still 5 hours later when they counted the last bill.

"That's one-point-seven," D-Lo said as he stashed the last bundle into the duffle bag.

"Fuck," Ghost stressed. He sat back on the couch, thinking.

"Wassup, bruh?"

"We down to our last two blocks and I still ain't met no fucking plug yet. Red still kickin' in on the gas but I can't find nothing on the work."

"Baby, I think I might have someone in mind," Tiffany said, sitting in Ghost's lap.

"Who?" he replied, looking at her suspiciously.

"Well, I met someone in Atlanta who introduced me to somebody else, who happens to be one of the biggest suppliers in the state."

"Set it up. I want to meet him tomorrow. Where is he?"

Tiffany looked at Ghost and smiled. "In Beverly Hills."

"This is too perfect." He beamed, rubbing his hands together.

"Do you think he'll supply us?" D-Lo asked curiously.

"Do you know who your little brother is?" Ghost returned sarcastically.

Everyone sat back and relaxed from the day through the night, waiting for morning to uphold. Ghost sat in the corner of the bed in the midst of his own thoughts. Mariah laid with her head against his thigh as Bernard laid to the right of him. He had come a long way from Simpson Road to meet his success. He thought about Erica and his skin crawled. The thought of having an FBI agent sleeping in his guest room was beyond weird, but the fact that she was his baby's mother was even weirder. He refused to walk away from the game without all the pieces to his puzzle. Even if it meant taking pieces off to make it fit.

A beautiful day filled the sky as Ghost, D-Lo, and Tiffany rode in the Maserati down to her supplier's house. As she pulled into the gate, four bodyguards surrounded the car.

One tapped the window. "How may I help you?" the bodyguard asked with a blank face.

"We have a meeting to see Pablo," Tiffany responded, looking the man in his eyes.

One of the bodyguards talked through his walkie talkie. After he got his response, he stepped out the way of the car and buzzed the gate open.

Riding inside of Pablo's parking lot looked like the entrance to Disney land. Forget a mansion. His house looked as if it was built off pictures of a castle.

Circling around the giant water fountain, Tiffany stopped the car and killed the engine. "Let's go," she said, looking at Ghost and D-Lo.

As they got out of the car, three more bodyguards approached them and started frisking Ghost and D-Lo. One guy tried to reach for Tiffany and Ghost grabbed his arm.

"Don't even fucking think about it, playboy," Ghost grimaced at the huge Spanish guy.

The man snatched his arm away from his grip as they stood in each other's faces.

"Chill, baby," Tiffany mouthed as she pulled Ghost towards the house.

Walking into the main entrance, Pablo sat in his wooden oak rocking chair with a glass of whiskey and a Cuban cigar in his mouth. "Hola, Tiffany, my beautiful princess. How are you?" Pablo greeted her as he stood.

"Hey, Pablo." Tiffany grinned.

"You are still young and precious. Why haven't I heard from you in so long?"

"You know me, Pablo, always on the move to make another dollar."

Pablo looked her in the eyes as he shook his head. "I see. You know if you ever need me, I'm only a phone call away."

"I know, Pablo."

"Who are your friends?" he asked, looking over at Ghost and D-Lo standing quietly.

"The name's Ghost. It's a pleasure to meet you." He nodded with his hand out.

"Ghost," Pablo repeated. "Very strong name. Our interpretation, where I'm from, it means the seat of life or intelligence. To move soft and quietly. Invincible." Pablo said, shaking Ghost's hand.

"I've heard that get shot at me a couple of times."

Tiffany sat down on the couch as Ghost began to talk to Pablo.

"And your name?" Pablo questioned, looking over at D-Lo.

"His name isn't important. I'm the one handling the business." Ghost stopped him, butting in.

Pablo looked at Tiffany then back at Ghost. "Okay, Mr. Ghost." Pablo chuckled. "I see you are very direct. What is it that I can do for you?"

"I need fifty keys of coke."

"Jeez, that's a lot of cociana, my friend. Things like that don't run cheap around the sunny side." Pablo spoke cautiously.

"Try me."

"Well, since you are trying to purchase so many, I could try and work it out for twelve a piece and that's really being generous, compodre."

"I was thinking on the borderline of like nine and I come get fifty every two weeks from you."

"Are you crazy? I have some of the purest coke you can find in these states."

"Good. That'll make it easier to sell it and I can come back every two weeks and buy at the same price." He returned arrogantly.

"Why would I give you keys for nine thousand dollars and I've never met you in my life? I don't even know anything about you, my friend," Pablo asked with honesty.

"Because, with all due respect, you will never meet a guy like me ever again. Money has no face on it Pablo. It's the person who's behind handling the paper. Now that will really assure you my money is good."

"And what if you can't complete the task?" Pablo asked, hitting his cigar.

"Then I will pay off the remaining three for each brick and never show my face around here again."

"I like him already," Pablo stated to Tiffany. "Come have a cigar with me, Ghost." He motioned as he stepped out in his backyard through the glass door.

Tiffany and D-Lo headed back to the car as Ghost and Pablo trailed the backyard. After he and Ghost shared a cigar, they discussed different prices and shook hands when coming to an agreement. When Ghost finally got in the car, Tiffany and D-Lo stared at him.

"What happened?" Tiffany asked, anxious to see what was going on.

"He told me he wants me to be his business partner. Something like an aggressor for people who can't act right. For that, I get 'em for nine apiece.

"Fucking right," D-Lo said, rubbing his hands together as he smiled from ear to ear.

"Baby, he must really like you. He used to charge me ten a key." She frowned from the love Pablo was showing him.

"What can I say, baby?" Ghost asked, kissing Tiffany. "I got a way with words."

Within the next six hours, Ghost and D-Lo pulled back in front of Pablo's house. After the trade was made, he shook hands with the boss man then he drove off as the new plug of California.

Ghost pushed his whip straight to the boondocks inside the pit of Los Angeles. After dropping the work off with the fam, the trap was back jumping. The streets were so thirsty that Ghost opened up two more spots and began to flood San Bernardino and even a little of Compton with Pablo's finest.

One week later

So many cars were parked at tonight's grand opening. The parking lot was flooded with foreign rides as more cars continued to enter. Tiffany ran through over 115 girls yesterday for the auditions. Only 26 women made the cut and were able to pass the test.

"Alright, ladies, listen up," Tiffany announced, sitting in the women's dressing room. "Please go out there and make me look good. I have picked you all and told my husband that y'all were the best. You're about to be a part of something that's gone be forever memorable. So, let's go shake some ass and make some bread."

The girls scrambled finishing their makeup.

First on stage was Honey. She was 5'9", and Amazon thick with blue eyes. Honey's real name was Selen, raised in the U.S but born in the Virgin Islands. Honey hypnotized the crowd as she stripped slowly, showing off her immaculate body. She stood on a handstand, hitting a split making, the crowd chunk their bankrolls on stage. Ghost sat back and watched as Honey did her thing. After her song was over, she disappeared to the back.

Next on stage was Tweety. She wasted no time in sticking her pussy towards a hood nigga's face. She grabbed her legs and made her ass cheeks jump one at a time. Tweety slid down to the ground, grabbing a bottle of Patron that was sitting on stage. She entered the bottle inside her pussy for a few seconds and snatched it out as liquor sprayed across the dance floor. The men were howling like dogs as Tweety continued to grind her hips to the beat. There was so much money on the stage you could barely see the floor. Tweety finished her song and blew Ghost a kiss as he clapped lightly at her performance. The club's music stayed amped as all twenty-six girls got out on stage and performed, making a killing.

Ghost sat back, watching and sipping his drink as Tiffany walked in front of him wearing her sexy, white Gucci dress.

"So, which ones do you want and how many," Tiffany asked seriously.

"What?" Ghost asked, looking at her awkwardly, thinking he didn't hear her correctly

"The girls, Ghost. We might as well do it now before they try and do it behind my back."

"Are you serious?"

Tiffany just stared at Ghost as the music boomed loudly threw the speakers

He looked into her eyes and saw that she was beyond playing. "Fuck it, I want all of em."

"All of them?" Tiffany spat with a little hatred in her voice.

"Yeah, might as well go all the way."

"Okay." Tiffany smacked her teeth as she walked off.

Chris Green

CHAPTER 5

"Ahh fuck," Honey moaned. She tried to eat Tiffany's pussy while Ghost fucked her from the back. He was sticking his thumbs in her ass as six other women licked on his neck, chest, and back.

The other women played with each other, switching positions, and Tiffany sat on Ghost's face while two other women began to put hickies on his stomach. Tweety rode Ghost, grinding his dick inside of her while another took his balls into her mouth. Tweety squatted over him, trying to take all of him like a big girl. She came down hard on his dick each time as Ghost met her thrust for thrust.

Tiffany already had cum twice thanks to the women hounding him. After Tweety got up, Fox, Coco, Lauren, and Cream all got on their knees as they began to attack Ghost with mouth after mouth.

"Fuck," Ghost moaned, sitting in heaven from all the mouths and hands that were pleasing him.

All the girls took turns putting Ghost's dick down their throat when they sucked on him slowly.

Fox was a caramel chick with a petite waist and frame. She walked over to Ghost and he bent her over, entering inside her. Her walls were tight and wet when her soppy pussy gripped Ghost's manhood. He gripped Fox's ass when her pussy farted back and forth as he pulled out of her.

Tiffany and Star made out as Fire buried her head in between Tiffany's legs. Ghost's manhood stood tall as he looked at Fires fat pussy when she bent over. He got up and walked behind her, entering her doggy style. He pumped inside her, trying to grip her soft ass that was sliding through his fingers. The pleasure from Ghost sliding inside her made the pussy eating session even better for Tiffany. He began to mash Fire's head into Tiffany's cookie as he went deeper inside her. Fire screamed Ghost's name out in pleasure, feeling him hit places inside her stomach she never knew existed. After having her third climax, Tiffany sat back and watched all the girls have their fun with Ghost. Their room was filled with varieties of appetites that turned into an orgy party. The session lasted until 3:30AM. Everyone passed out where ever they could.

Ghost rolled over out of his bed, letting his feet touch the floor. He fired up his blunt as he slid on his sweat pants. He politely stretched his arms, stepping over all the women to go check on the kids.

Mariah laid next to D-Lo in the bed while Laylah rested in her crib sound asleep. Ghost closed the door and headed downstairs in search of his son. Erica laid stretched out on a pallet with Bernard next to her.

Ghost picked up his son and kissed Erica on the cheek, waking her up. "Why you ain't in the bed?" He asked, leading her to the guest room. He laid his son on the bed and stripped Erica out of her clothes. After he wrapped the cover around her he kissed her lips.

"Ghost, do you still love me?"

"Of course, I do."

"Like when we first met," Erica replied trying to read him.

"No. I love you more than when I first met you." He sat on the bed as he massaged her thighs and feet until she drifted back to sleep.

Ghost then crept out of the bedroom and headed in the kitchen where he began to make a hot pot of coffee. As he poured the mixture into the strainer his phone vibrated with a text message from Dillon.

"Turn to CNN," he read the message out loud.

He walked to the cabinet drawer, grabbing the remote to the fifty-inch plasma, and turned on the TV.

"In the creek behind the apartments of Collier Heights, Notorious gang member Fando Mitchell, AKA Flame, was found with four gunshot wounds to the back of the head. His hands were severed from the wrists down, and his feet were handcuffed. Detectives discovered an ace of spade playing card in the victim's back pocket, and are still waiting for more evidence at this time. According to detectives, Mitchell was a bodyguard for a drug dealer who was gunned down seven months ago in southwest Atlanta. Investigators say it was retaliation for having his boss set-up, but there are still no leads."

Ghost cut the TV off after listening to the story. He knew Twan wasn't set up because he murdered him personally. And for somebody to kill his bodyguard meant that someone wanted some answers.

Looks like a nigga finally want to get some straightening about that nigga, Ghost thought.

Tiffany walked through the kitchen. All the girls followed suit and kissed Ghost's right cheek.

"What y'all about to do?" He asked, looking at all of the women.

"I'm 'bout to fix these girls some breakfast and they're gonna head out so they can get ready for work tonight."

"Okay," Ghost replied, nodding his head in approval.

"And let me tell all y'all bitches something now. If I catch you fucking my man without my permission, I'm gonna try my best to feed you every bullet I got," Tiffany said, turning back around to the stove.

Tweety tooted her lips as she winked at Ghost. He smiled as he walked over to Tiffany, grabbing her by the waist. He sat her on top of the counter.

"Baby, what are you doing?"

Ghost got on his knees, sliding her shorts to the side as he licked her love button. Tiffany jolted her head back as Ghost's tongue polluted her mind instantly. The girls' mouths sat wide open as Ghost continued to spread her lips apart. He slowly sucked every ounce of wetness out of her while massaging her clit.

"Fuck, baby, stoppp!" Tiffany moaned, grabbing the back of Ghost's head.

When Ghost started to feel Tiffany's leg shake, he fixed her shorts and helped her off the counter. "You can't ever think a bitch can amount to you, bae." He smiled, licking his fingers as he walked off.

The girls stared in amazement as half of the women's pussies thumped with anticipation.

"Somebody help me cook breakfast." Tiffany shook, looking embarrassed.

"You might need to have a seat sweetie," Honey said as all the girls giggled.

Erica began to smell the masterpiece that was cooking as it ran through her nostrils. She got out of bed, slid on her clothes and headed to the kitchen. She wondered what Ghost was cooking as she walked through the massive entrance. Seeing the large group of women in the room, Erica turned around to walk out.

"Where are you going?" Tiffany asked her.

"Umm. I just thought Ghost was making breakfast for everyone. I didn't mean to interrupt."

"You ain't interrupting shit. Come sit down. Girls, this is Ghost's baby mother and girlfriend."

The girls looked at each other awkwardly as Tiffany fixed a cup of coffee and passed it to Erica.

"So, basically, she's a sideline bitch." Co-Co said, trying to be funny and get on Tiffany's good side.

All the girls began to laugh as Tiffany looked over at Co-Co with an ugly frown.

"No, I'm not a sideline bitch." Erica said, looking at Co-Co. "I'm his child's mother, and I'll appreciate it if you mind your own fucking business and stay out of ours."

"I'm sorry," Co-Co apologized. "I didn't mean to be funny. I was just acknowledging the real head chick of the household, not the nanny."

Before Co-co could say another word. Erica jumped across the table, smashing the glass cup across her head. As she fell to the floor, Erica grabbed Co-Co's hair and kneed her four times, splitting her eye and nose. All the girls jumped out of the way in shock as Erica demolished Co-Co inside the wide kitchen.

Tiffany continued to cook breakfast as she watched the girl get her ass beat. The commotion was so loud that D-Lo and Suave walked in on Erica blacking out.

"Oh shit," Suave said laughing. "What the hell she done did?"

Ghost walked into the kitchen to witness Co-Co balled up on the floor as Erica kicked her repeatedly. "What the hell is wrong with you?" Ghost asked, grabbing Erica's neck, making her look at him.

The tight grip on her throat instantly cut off her air supply as she began to pour tears.

"Ghost, let her go, Co-Co started it with her," Tiffany shouted, seeing Ghost overreact.

He quickly released his grip to have Erica run out of the kitchen to the bedroom. "What the fuck is going on?" He yelled, watching the girls help Co-Co off the floor.

"Co-Co disrespected that girl for no reason. And if you ask me, I'll say she deserved everything that just happened." Tiffany said, turning back around to the stove.

"Co-Co, get ya' shit and go, be at the club tonight to clear ya' locker out. You're fired." Ghost spat as he walked out of the kitchen.

Co-Co gave him an evil stare as Tweety grabbed her things to escort her out to the car.

"Do you want me to drive you to the hospital," Tweety asked Co-Co with a worried expression.

"No," Co-Co shouted slamming her car door.

"Girl, you have some serious injuries, let me take you to the doctor."

Co-Co crank her car up and pulled off. While driving down the street, she reached for her cellphone and began to place a call.

"Yo," the male said on the other side of the phone.

"Baby, I know where that nigga at."

"Oh yeah?" he said. "And where is that?"

"Cali," Co-Co uttered.

When he heard the word Cali, he pushed the strippers head from his lap and buried his ear closer to the phone. "Say that again?"

"He's in California, close to Beverly Hills."

The man flashed a crooked smile and hung up the phone. Firing up his cigarette, Bullshit looked at the front of his screensaver on the phone. His cousin was on the reign to taking over the whole city until Ghost took him away. As he stood up off the couch, he plotted and envisioned how he would blow Ghost's brains out.

"Yoo, Five," Bullshit said, banging on the bedroom door.

"Yo, come in, nigga."

Bullshit walked in the room as Shooter fucked Tyra from the back. "Man, what the fuck, slime," Bullshit said, turning his head.

"Nigga, what the fuck poppin'? You just gone stand there?" Shooter asked as he looked back.

"They found that nigga, bro."

"Who?"

"That nigga Ghost." Bullshit's eyes focused on his screen as he scrolled past a picture of P in his gallery.

Shooter stopped ramming Tyra as he looked back at Bullshit. "Are you serious?"

"Why would I play?" He calmly stated, walking out of the room.

Convinced that Bullshit wasn't kidding, Shooter pushed Tyra away from him as he slid inside his pants and shoes. Walking into his closet, he grabbed his two Beretta 9-millimeters and a silver suitcase. Then, he headed towards the living room. "So, where the fuck are we going?" He asked Bullshit.

"We're going home."

Shooter sat back and balanced the words in his head that he was just told. "You mean to tell me this nigga is in Cali?"

Bullshit looked over at him and grinned as he placed his hat over his curly hair.

"I guess this finna be a crazy fucking reunion," Shooter said as he gathered his things.

Bullshit nodded as they headed for the door.

Tragedy was on its way to Cali and the devil laid in wait for bullshit at all times.

As Ghost walked in the room, Erica sat staring out of the window holding Bernard in her hands. Tears streamed down her face as he walked in front of the bed, lifting her head.

"Why is the dream we had for our life slowly drifting away? Why can't we be gracious for the things we already have?" Erica asked as her face glistened with tears.

Ghost looked at her and saw the hurt and pain running through her veins. He kneeled down in front of her and kissed he lips. "Trials and tribulations are never meant to last forever. Soon we will be able to live and forget about shit that never mattered anyways. Keep your head focused on the objective." Ghost responded, wiping her tears away.

"Whoa, my brother," Suave said, clutching his pistol as he looked out of the blinds.

"Wassup, Don?" D-Lo greeted him, though he was Face Timing his girl.

"Come check this out real quick, bro."

"Let me hit you back, ma." D-Lo put the iPad down onto the table and made his way to the window. "What the hell you see?"

"Look, nigga," Suave stressed, pointing at the pool cleaners van that sat four houses down.

"What? The pool van?" D-Lo asked confusingly.

He closed his eyes and shook his head in silence.

"What about it?"

"What type of pool cleaners van got a satellite on top of the roof?"

D-Lo thought about it and stared at the van for a second, while still looking at Suave out the corner of his eye.

He began bursting out in laughter as he held Suave's shoulder. "Bro, stop smoking so much gas nigga, you just paranoid."

"I will stop killing for a month if that's a pool cleaner." Suave said, holding out his hand.

"Yeah right, nigga. That's like you telling me not to fuck the pussy and I'm in the room with six naked women."

"And if it is them folks, then what?" Suave countered.

"Then I'll give you ten bands."

"Come on."

After walking out of the door, Suave went down the steps and across the street to knock on the window of the van.

The pool man jumped, looking to his side seeing Suave standing at the window. "How may I help you sir," the man asked nervously.

"Yeah, how much y'all niggas be charging to clean these big ass pools out?" Suave asked aggressively.

"Depends on how big it is, sir, but you would have to set up an appointment." The pool cleaner then crank up the van.

Suave sensed the fear from him, though the man tried to avoid eye contact. "Shit, why you can't come and check it out now?"

"I'm sorry sir, but I already have an appointment that I have to be getting to across town. Good day." The man pulled out of the neighborhood.

D-Lo was crouched behind a can as the van pulled off without anyone noticing.

"Did you get it on there?"

D-Lo shook his head as he analyzed the whole scenario in the back of his brain.

"Oh, my fucking God," Agent Ross said, taking off his cleaner's shirt. "Do you think they caught on to us?" he asked Agent Moore, who was in the back of the van. "I can't believe we were just that close to that psychopathic motherfucker, and we still haven't even spotted our suspect. Let's just get back to headquarters and wait until we can come up with a little more info before we call the director back."

D-Lo pulled the wad of money out of his pocket and handed it to Suave as they listened to the two agents through the device he placed at the bottom of the van, thanks to Shadow. Now that their investigation was out the bag, the plan was to lead them to exactly who they wanted. Ghost.

CHAPTER 6

The black SUV came to a halt directly at the center of the house, which was Ghost's trap. A white male with a leather trench coat stepped from behind the car with the sun beaming on his black shades in the early afternoon. He walked up the driveway to the front door, then knocked on the burglar bars.

"Yoo, who the fuck is it?" J.L. asked, getting off the floor with the breezy he caught from the club last night.

"Probably Ghost ass," Tim said as he puffed on his Newport.

Without looking, J.L. opened the door. As he unlocked the gate, three shots rang out. Two hit him directly in the shoulder. The third bullet struck a wall as the white man walked in the house, shooting at everything he could see.

Tim jumped off the couch, snatching his 40 from his waist. He let off round after round as the man backed away, releasing his gun. A bullet struck the girl in the head when she tried to scramble from the floor. Tim ducked behind the mini bar breathing hard as the killer sprayed and riddled the wall with bullets.

He jumped up, catching the man in his chest twice. The killer's gun let loose, piercing Tim in the stomach. Tim fell first against the wall, dropping his gun as the hitman fell to the floor. Tim slowly gained his composure, holding his hand over his wound and picked up his gun. He came up around the bar stumbling as he walked over to J.L.

"Bruh, you good, my nigga?"

"Yeah, I can't move, dog. Call the ambulance." J.L. said as he closed his eyes, trying to ease the pain.

"Just hold on, bruh."

He walked over to the man who was breathing erratically and looked at him with death running through his aura. Tim grunted, aiming his gun in the man's face. "Who sent you?"

"Fuck you," the hitman cursed with blood starting to the surface of his mouth.

"That's right, pussy nigga, fuck this," Tim gritted before placing four shots into the man's face.

Dropping his gun on the floor, Tim dug in his pocket for his phone and dialed 911.

After he placed the call to the paramedics, he used the last of his energy to dial Ghost's number on his dial pad.

"Whoa?" Ghost answered the phone as he sat on the couch with Erica.

"Don, we need ya' help," Tim tried to speak beginning to become dizzy. He leaned against the wall and clutched on to his stomach from the tremendous amount of blood he was losing.

"What's going on?" Ghost placed the phone closer to his ear, feeling something was wrong. "Don, what's going on?"

"We got shot up, bruh… the spot." Was all Tim got to say before he collapsed on the floor.

"Hello?" Ghost shouted, leaning up.

"Baby, what's wrong?" Erica asked.

Jumping off of the couch, he grabbed his gun and headed towards the door.

D-Lo watched his brother's movements. He grabbed the AR-15, then they climbed in the car and swerved off.

Thirty minutes later, Ghost swerved on the street the spot sat on. Seeing the paramedics bring out a stretcher with a bloody body atop it, his heart skipped a beat. He felt the current of rage as he stopped the officer walking in front of the car.

"Sir, what occurred over here?" Ghost asked, sticking his head out the window like a worried citizen.

"There was a horrible shooting. Two homicides." The officer said with his hand on his gun.

"Where are the victims that were in the house?" Ghost asked impatiently.

"They were transferred to the nearest hospital."

Ghost stuck his head back in the window, headed down the street to Martin Luther King's community hospital. He floored his pedal non-stop until he reached the parking lot.

He hopped out of the car and found the front desk. "Excuse me ma'am, you just had two people come in from a shooting. What rooms are they in?" Ghost asked eagerly.

"They're in rooms five and six. Do you have a valid ID that I can verify?" The nurse asked as D-Lo and Ghost walked away from her. "Sir, you all just can't walk back there." The nurse picked up the phone as she watched them go into the first room.

Ghost looked at Tim laying in the hospital bed motionless. He walked over beside him as he breathed harshly through the oxygen ventilator. His mind went into override when seeing his friend as stiff as a coffin.

D-Lo was about to speak when a bald headed white male came through the door, wearing a white over coat.

"Hi, I'm doctor McClair," the man greeted them, holding his hand out.

"What's going on with him?" Ghost shouted, getting close to the doctor's face.

"Ghost, chill," D-Lo said, grabbing his younger brother after seeing the doctor tense up.

"Well, he's been shot, sir. The bullet pierced his lung, striking a main artery. He would have bled to death if we wouldn't have gotten there when we did. He's hurt bad but he will live. Worst case, he might have to wear a colostomy bag or temporarily use a wheel chair. I'm not sure yet," the doctor said sternly.

"Whatever you have to do to make sure he's in top notch health, I want it done. Any medical expense can be taken care of."

"Yes, sir, I'll make sure he's in the best of care."

Ghost and D-Lo walked out of Tim's room and entered J.L.'s next door. As they inched into the room, he opened his eyes to see his brothers.

"You a'ite, my nigga?" Ghost asked, looking into his eyes.

Licking his dry lips, J.L. shook his head as he tried to maintain the pain. "Shots just started coming out of nowhere, dog. I didn't have time to do nothing, bro. Nigga just cut me down bad." J.L. grunted as he looked at Ghost.

"What did this motherfucker look like?" D-Lo asked with a lot of aggravation.

"A white man, dog, he had shades and a trench coat on. Whoever he was, he didn't come to play. Luckily Tim could move better than me, ya' know."

"Who else was in the house, bro?" Ghost asked J.L.

"Just me, Tim, and my lil' breezy, dog. She didn't make it, though."

"Where is she from?" Ghost raised his eyebrow.

"She stays in that last house on the end of Piru Street."

"Do you know who stay with her?" D-Lo asked.

"Her mom and little brother, some little blood nigga about eighteen years old." Julian said, trying to remember.

D-Lo and Ghost looked over at each other as they listened to him closely.

"Rest up, my nigga. We gone make sure you good," D-Lo spoke.

"Where's Tim, dog?" J.L.'s voice shook.

"He's fine, my nigga. You just worry about healing up. Everything gone be good."

When Ghost and D-Lo walked out of the hospital room, they ran into three security guards and two detectives who waited quietly in the hallway.

"Mr. Grey, how are you?" The male detective greeted Ghost as he entered his personal space a little too much.

"Not too fucking good, and how the fuck do you know my name?" Ghost asked cautiously.

"I'm detective Welch, and this is my assistant, Detective Beckett."

"And?" He replied with an 'I don't give a fuck' face.

"Well, sir, since we have you proceeding back and forth from that little crack house of yours, do you know the reason it got riddled with bullets today?" Detective Welch prodded.

"I don't know what the fuck you're talking about!"

"Oh, you don't know, huh? Let me tell you something, you motherfucker. I know who you are, Mr. Ghost. You think you're gonna try to come to my city without me knowing, and do what you did to Atlanta, huh? You've been tied to over fourteen murders in the past six years and still seem to slip through the cracks. But me, personally, I will be on your ass every step of the way. You won't be able to take a shit without me knowing what you ate for breakfast. Any place you think that you can go without me knowing, I'll be creeping, waiting for you to slip like a punk ass, crackhead whore who had a fucking relapse. Ya' hear me?" Detective Welch said, looking determined.

Ghost eyed the detective and spit on the floor next to his shoes. "You know what they say, detective. You can only keep putting your hand in the pit bull's bowl for so long until he bites. Besides that, have a good day, pig." Ghost and D-Lo walked past the five officers.

"What you think, bruh?" D-Lo asked as they made their way into the parking lot.

"I don't know, bruh. These folks obviously been watching too hard. We can't slip and let these folks catch us down. We need some pawn workers, fast. At least until I figure out what's going on."

"What about J.L. and Tim?"

"We go out hunting tonight and make somebody snitch on their friend."

As they jumped in the car and pulled off, Ghost thought about how it actually may have to get dangerous in California. But what he didn't know was the enemy wouldn't stop until he was dead.

Erica and Tiffany sat in the house with Mariah, Bernard and Laylah. They both jumped to their feet when hearing Ghost swerve back into the parking lot.

"Oh my God, Ghost, what's going on?" Erica asked when Ghost walked through the door.

"A lot!" He said, then kissed Erica and Tiffany. He walked over and gave kisses to Mariah, Bernard and Laylah.

"Ghost, what the hell is going on? You're scaring me." Tiffany asked, standing in front of him.

"I'll be back. Do you have your gun?" Ghost asked.

"Yeah, its upstairs. What's going on?"

Ghost took a deep breath. "I think my little beef from Atlanta has caught up with us."

"What do you need us to do?" Tiffany asked.

"I need y'all to lay low with the kids. Shadow will be close around, watching out for you all. Erica, do you have your gun?" Ghost asked her.

"Yeah, I got it," Erica replied, fidgeting as she pulled her 380 out of her ankle holster.

"Cool, I want you both to lock the door and stay with the kids. Where is Suave?"

"He's at the club tonight, baby. Tonight was on him for management."

"Just keep y'all eyes open. Tomorrow we gone relocate to Erica's house and only conduct business from here. I have to make sure y'all and the kids are completely safe. If anyone tries to come in the house, kill 'em, no questions asked." Ghost said as he walked out of the door.

Getting to the truck, D-Lo opened it, grabbing his glocc 19 and the MP5 as Ghost grabbed his pearl handled glocc 40. After they strapped on their vest, D-Lo got in the driver's seat as Ghost quietly got in the passenger.

"Take us back to Piru Street." Ghost said as he rested his head on the seat.

Devon sat outside on the front of his porch with two of his gang brothers and a little thot who loved to hang around.

"Yo, blood, I'm telling you, when I find out who had something to do with my sister getting murdered, it's gone be popping, ASAP, ya' feel me?"

"We heard about that. Whose spot she was in when that shit happened?" The boy with the red bandana on his head asked.

"Some new niggas on the block. I think them pussies from Atlanta. They lucky they got wet up 'cause I woulda been gunning at them lames about my sister."

Ghost and D-Lo sat at the end of the block with their lights off as they watched the group on the porch. Opening their doors they slowly got out of the car and made their way to the house.

The teenagers were so deep into their conversation they never paid attention to D-Lo putting the silenced pistol to one of the young boy's head before splattering his brains across Devon's face.

"What the fuck, man?" Devon yelled in fear as he watched D-Lo knock the other kid's bandana and face into the front yard.

"What's hannin', lil' nigga?" Ghost asked, putting his gun to Devon's face.

"Who da fuck are you, bro?" He squealed, shaking like a stripper as he wiped the blood off his face.

"I'm the nigga that's finna dome call yo' stupid ass and send ya' home with ya' sister if I don't get the right answers."

"About what?" The fear began to kick in strong as his knees was about to give out and buckle as he looked Ghost in the eyes.

"How long has yo' sister been fucking with them nigga's asses down the street?"

"For like a week or something. I don't know."

"So, who da fuck would know something then, nigga?" Ghost was getting mad.

"I don't know what you mean, man," Devon replied with his hands in the air.

"I mean, who the fuck is the big dog out here callin' shots?" He spoke harshly pointing his pistol in between the young boy's eyes.

"Man, my brother runs this block, blood. He down in Atlanta right now. I promise I don't know what happened. Come on man, my sister got killed. If I knew something I would tell you." Devon said, closing his eyes so he wouldn't have to look down the barrel of the gun.

"What's ya' brother's name, blood?"

"My brother's name is Bullshit, man."

Ghost's aura instantly changed when hearing the name. His mind went blank as he looked at who he was standing in front of. "Do me a favor. When you see your brother, tell 'em Ghost looking for him, and I'm not your blood, pussy." Ghost spat before he shot Devon in between his eyes, watching his body crumble to the floor.

The old woman across the street stepped back into her house when she saw a child she raised up from birth get murdered. The girl balled up in the corner as Ghost turned around looking at her.

As they headed off the porch to the corner, the LA police pulled up to an immediate halt in front of Ghost and D-Lo. The police jumped out with their guns drawn.

"Freeze, motherfuckers! Put your hands in the air!" The officer demanded.

D-Lo and Ghost stood froze. D-Lo looked at him and nodded his head as they began letting shots off at the officers and ducking for cover. The two law officials returned fire as they took cover behind the parked cars and traded bullets back and forth.

Ghost held his position behind the car as D-Lo ducked low by his side. The gunshots penetrated the vehicle's window and doors as the officer's released their guns.

Ghost nodded his head as D-Lo stood, firing his gun and hitting one of the officers, taking off his left jaw. He ducked back down swiftly as the officer began to let his clip ride and call for back up.

"Go," Ghost whispered to D-Lo, pointing at the car.

"I can't leave you, nigga, let's go together."

"This the only way we gone make it outta here if you trust me. I gotta distract him. Just fucking go, nigga," Ghost motioned, looking at him as if he was wasting time.

D-Lo looked at his little brother and dashed for the car. As he jumped in, he crank up the whip and swerved off. The officer jumped from behind the cruiser, letting shots go, shattering the back window.

Boc! Boc! Boc! Boc! Boc!

The officer continued shooting until D-Lo sped around the corner, disappearing into the night. Running back to his partner's side, he tried to stop the blood as he kneeled down over him. "Come on, Larry, stay with me," the officer said as the blood soaked up his hands and uniform.

"So, who gone do CPR for you, pig ass nigga?" Ghost asked, putting his gun to the back of the officer's head.

He closed his eyes, knowing that he made the biggest mistake of not keeping his eyes on his perimeter.

"Checkmate, fuckman," Ghost said, hitting the officer in the back of his head twice, leaving him on top of his partner's body.

He ran and jumped in the police car as he smashed the gas, hitting the sirens. He turned the music up to the max as he made a right by Towne Street, and almost side-swiped a car. He swerved through traffic and ran every red light he saw as he smashed the pedal to the floor. Pulling out his phone, his finger pressed the dial button and called D-Lo.

"Whoa, where the fuck are you, Ghost?" D-Lo asked quietly.

"I'm cruising through the streets in my six-four, nigga," Ghost shouted, smiling.

"What?"

Ghost shook his head. "Come and get me. I'ma be behind the warehouse down the street from Crenshaw." Ghost hung up.

As he turned into the dead-end of the warehouse, he mashed the gas up to 100 miles per hour and jumped out, rolling across the ground. The police cruiser slammed into the building, exploding as it hit the toxic chemicals on the inside.

Ghost watched as the car burned and smiled, knowing it was time to release the devil upon California.

Chris Green

CHAPTER 7

As night time drifted and it rolled over to morning, Ghost laid in the bed with Tiffany. His phone rang.

"Hello?" Ghost answered in a groggy voice with his eyes still closed.

"Hola, Ghost. It is important that I speak with you."

"I'm listening, Pablo," he replied.

Pablo laughed lightly into the phone. "I have been doing this a very long time, Ghost. The way I move is precise and strategic. I will see you in my backyard in thirty minutes," Pablo demanded, hanging up.

Ghost looked at the phone as if he wanted to sling it out of the room. He looked over at Tiffany. She looked like a trophy wife wrapped in the covers. He kissed her soft lips and grabbed her butt as he held her firmly. After sitting in the bed for two minutes, he got up and applied on his gear. He dressed in his Balmain biker rib jeans, Balmain t-shirt and a black Spurs snapback. After he laced up his all white Air Force Ones, he grabbed his gun and tucked it in his waistline, then exited out of the bedroom. Stopping in the living area, Ghost walked to the guest bedroom and kissed Mariah, Erica and Bernard. Finally, he left out of the house.

After hopping in his car, he drove for the next 25 minutes until he reached Pablo's parking lot. As Sanchez buzzed Ghost through the gate, he looked at all the exquisite things Pablo's mansion obtained.

He knew that for a fact he was going to reach that level. He was already a millionaire but the money meant nothing. Ghost could easily kill and take money for the rest of his life if he wanted. It was the power that he truly desired.

Stepping out of the car, he was escorted to the backyard where Pablo sat in a lawn chair next to his crystal, sea blue pool. Ghost walked over and treated himself to a big cigar, and took his seat next to Pablo's.

"So, wassup, Pab," Ghost said as he fired up his cigar, looking over at him.

"If I told you it was ten million dollars at the bottom of that pool, would you jump in to get it?" Pablo asked, puffing on his cigar.

"Hell yeah, no questions asked."

"But what if the pool wasn't crystal clear to see inside? What if it was dark and black as the night? Would you still go in?" Pablo said, flipping his question.

Looking at the sky-blue pool, he thought before he answered. "As long as I know it's down there, I wouldn't give a fuck what color it is, Pablo."

"My point is, many people would have to see things in order for them to believe it. You are a winner because you are willing to take chances that not too many people will take. Seeing a box full of money in crystal blue water would make anyone jump in just to get their hands on the prize. But if you have a black pool with a case full of money in it, people would be less interested because of what their eyes don't see. You are a chance taker and only people who take chances win without a doubt."

Ghost put out his cigar as he soaked Pablo's words in like a sponge.

"Loyalty, Ghost, is the reason why men like us are fortunate and last long, my friend. A man will do whatever it takes to make it to the top. Even if it means to knock down all competition and competitors. They are better when they can't compete at all. Knowledge is sometimes given to a brain that doesn't know how to put the knowledge in effect. Certain people have the wisdom to operate without needing further knowledge from what history has shown them. Always let your past speak from your present, Ghost, and there is no limit to what you can do, my friend." Pablo took a sip of his whiskey.

"So, what about you, Pablo? When are you gonna start to let your history speak instead of your present being in control."

"Ghost, soon I will be too old to do anything. Soon, all of this that's mine will belong to someone else, and soon my legacy will be in the hands of a strong enough person who can rule with an iron fist. I say that to say, never let it control you, but better if you can control it." Pablo pulled a key from his neck and handed it to Ghost. "There is a case in your trunk that contains a hundred kilos of cocaine. Nine of every key is mine and the rest is the start of your empire."

As Ghost sucked in all the words that he was given, he really knew that Pablo respected his ambition.

"There are better keys that I hold for you, Ghost, but will you let it control you or grasp it and place control of it?" Pablo stood, embraced him in a firm hug and looked at him. "Succeed until I'm no longer here, Ghost. Take my blessing to reign supreme."

Ghost smiled at Pablo as he sparked his cigar back up. "My life has been built off reigning, Pablo. Motivation has to start off as a seed to process towards dedication. It's something I've never lost or forgotten. Thank you."

Pablo nodded his head in silence.

Ghost walked back through the house to his car. He recollected on his way back to the crib. He thought about Pablo's words as they daggered through his brain. He wondered, was Pablo actually trying to leave his wealth with him? Pablo was one of the richest cocaine sealers in American. His connections were beyond unreachable and his net worth was every bit of $400 million. Pablo was powerful, and just being in his presence made Ghost appreciative.

Pulling into a corner store, Ghost stopped to grab him a pack of White Owl blunts. Getting out of the car, he thought about the last few years of his life and everything that played a part in him winning. His life was great. He was a millionaire. He had two beautiful women. He had three wonderful children, and his whole team was eating.

As Ghost walked, not paying attention to where he was going, he bumped into the back of a man while the man talked to two more guys in the parking lot.

"Damn, my bad bro," Ghost said as he tried to walk pass the men.

"Man, what the fuck? You blind or somethin', duck ass nigga?" The dark skin man shouted.

"He gotta be," the shorter of the three cut in, co-signing.

Ghost rubbed the bridge of his nose as he thought about blowing the man's brains out, but kept his composure and continued walking into the store.

After purchasing all the things he needed, he grabbed his bag and walked back out of the building. When he came around the corner, the three young dudes were posted on the hood of his Maserati. Ghost's temper instantly began to flair as he walked over towards his ride.

"You fuck niggas got five seconds to get the fuck off my car, or I'ma put one of you bitch's brains on the windshield."

The three dudes must have had a lot of heart because when he made his comment, they all busted out in laughter.

Ghost pulled out his 40, slapping the little one in his face, making him hit the ground.

"Un-uh," the dark skin man said, whipping his pistol out in Ghost's face.

Ghost smiled at him and the men leveled their pistol in each other's vision. "I don't think neither one of you street punk fags ready to die today." Ghost said with his foot on the short man's throat.

"I don't think you the only nigga with a strap, shawty," the man chuckled as he and Ghost itched to pull on their triggers.

Ghost lowered his gun and removed his foot off the young dude's neck. Jumping off the ground, the boy pulled his gun out. Before he could point it at Ghost, he removed it from his hand and broke it down in seconds. He dropped the pieces of the gun on the ground. The young dude backed away with his hand holding his neck. The other two sat back and watched as they realized Ghost wasn't just the average person.

"Where the fuck are you nigga's from?" Ghost asked, looking at them crazy.

The three men looked at each other as they all shared a laugh.

"What type of crazy ass question is that? We from the city, bruh," the dark skin cat said arrogantly.

"So, what's the reason for being in California?"

"We just up here for a funeral. One of my rich ass uncles' bitches ass passed away. We tearing it down out this weak ass state and heading back to Atlanta in a few days. The name's Tay, bruh," the dark skin one said, giving Ghost some dap.

"My name is Trouble, my nigga," the light skin, quiet man said coolly, saluting Ghost.

"Yeah nigga, and my motherfucking name is Woodie, and we gone have some damn problems the next time you hit me in my mouth like that too," the shorter one said, shaking hands with Ghost.

He laughed as he looked at the guys who kind of reminded him of his crew and himself when he was a couple years younger. "Do you niggas even got some paper in ya' pocket?" Ghost teased, looking at all three of them.

"I guess I do," Tay said as he pulled a few thousands out of his pocket and started thumbing through it.

Woodie did the same with the $600 in his pocket like it was really more. And Trouble just looked at Ghost as if he was insulted that he even asked the question.

"Y'all niggas hop in," Ghost said, unlocking the doors.

After all four men jumped in the car, he pulled off, heading towards the house.

Riding through Beverly Hills was a real scene. The three men looked out the window as the houses went from big to humongous. The deeper they went, the more luxurious and expensive the houses became.

"Boy, you definitely not finna see no shit like this in the city. Campbellton is all I know," Tay said, looking back and forth at all the properties.

Ghost's eyes trailed over to Tay. "You from Campbellton?"

"Hell yeah. Campbellton's finest."

"So, you blood?" Ghost asked, smiling

Tay's face balled up into a frown hearing Ghost's words. He shook his head as the threw up two big C's.

"Oh, you crip?"

"To death, my boy. The crip shit the best way," Tay bragged, rubbing his ball head.

"My bad, homie." Ghost prayed, but he was thankful that he didn't have to murder him inside his whip.

"None taken. So, spill the beans. You definitely got to have something going on if you're swerving through Beverly Hills. This shit ain't nothing but some good M's. So, what you got in yo' wallet?"

Ghost chuckled because he knew what Tay said was true. "Yeah, I got a lil' somethin', but I worked hard for it, and remained loyal to myself and my family. Trust me, it'll get you a long way." Ghost said with his eyes on the road.

"Yeah true, but in order to have loyalty, you gotta put it in effect to. Some just feel like they are loyal, when in reality they don't even know what it is."

Ghost pondered on Tay's words and felt exactly where he was coming from. He continued to push his whip as he looked in the rearview at Trouble and Woodie. "How do y'all nigga's hustle?"

"How don't we hustle? Weed, robbing, crack, pimping. You name it, we done it." Trouble said proudly.

"Finessing," Tay slid in with a smile on his face.

They all shared a laugh.

Pulling on Oakhurst Drive, Ghost parked in the parking lot of the house. All the boys got out, admiring how big it was.

"Nigga, how much this shit run?" Woodie asked.

They all walked up the steps to the house.

"Two-point-three million," Ghost responded as he stuck the key in the door. He opened it and walked in.

When they all stepped inside the house, Tiffany laid across the couch in a pair of white booty shorts, a tight white V neck shirt and a pair of pink high-top socks that came over her thighs. Her hair was pulled back into a pony tail while she watched the 60-inch plasma in the living room.

"Come on, follow me," Ghost said.

They began to walk towards his Round Table room.

"Hold up," Woodie said, walking over to Tiffany. "Damn baby, can I learn a little bit about you?"

Tiffany laughed at Woodie, who couldn't possibly know she was the Queen to the devil himself. She stood up as her ass crack devoured her shorts and walked over to Ghost. "Hi baby," Tiffany grinned as she began tonguing Ghost down and grabbing his dick through his pants. "Who're your dumb little friends?" she asked, looking at all of them with a blank expression.

"This is Tay, that's Trouble right there, and this young lunatic right here is Woodie." Ghost replied, shaking his head.

"Hmmm, okay. When you get done with these boring ass boys, can you come dig in this pussy for mama? It misses you." Tiffany whispered, licking the side of Ghost neck.

Ghost smiled at Tiffany, then softly kissed her lips. "I'll be there in a second."

As she walked off elsewhere, Ghost continued to head towards the office. Walking in, Shadow, D-Lo and Suave passed around a blunt as they discussed business about the recent profits and spots.

"Whoa, what the fuck mobbing?" Ghost greeted them as he showed all of his brothers some love.

"Uh, who the fuck are they?" Shadow asked, staring at the crew he had with him.

"This is Tay."

"What's hannin'," Tay said with a salute.

"This is Trouble. and this is Woodie," Ghost introduced the boys to his brothers.

"Oh okay, wassup guys?" Shadow asked with a smile. "But who the fuck are they?"

Ghost shook his head, knowing Shadow didn't like them already. "We happened to have a little dispute at the liquor store earlier, but they turned out to be some good people."

"Oh, that's wonderful man, I'm glad that worked out for you guys. But why the fuck are they here?"

"I don't think we would be here if your homie didn't want us here, my boy," Tay said, feeling Shadow's vibe of dislike.

"Now who in the fuck asked you anything, potna?" Shadow asked, sliding a bullet in the chamber of his handgun.

"Shit, the same person running they mouth, my nigga," Tay shot back, sliding his gun off his waist.

Trouble inched for his gun and Suave stood up, pointing his pistol in between his eyes. In the blink of an eye, D-Lo, Suave and Shadow stood off with Tay, Trouble and Woodie.

Ghost stood in the middle of them with his hands on his forehead. He instantly regretted bringing the young heads to meet the fam. "How about all y'all niggas chill out and put the guns down?"

"I think these babies tryna get spanked," Shadow said, still pointing his gun forcefully.

"Let's just chill and sit the fuck down." Ghost was trying to ease the tension.

"I'm gone handle you. Pulling that strap out and not using it, bitch," Shadow mumbled to Tay as he eased back in the chair at the table.

Tay and his boys lowered their weapons out of respect for Ghost. Suave and D-Lo did the same.

"Now you niggas supposed to be Dons, so how are you acting Mafioso right now?"

"Exactly," Ghost said as the room sat in silence. He pulled his pearl handled glocc from his waist and turned to Tay and his crew. "How about we go ahead and get straight down to the business and the point. Either you niggas want to make some money or not. If you do want to make this paper, you guys will be labeled The Black Team and you hustle and kill when the time is necessary. Capeesh? You all would be taken care of to the fullest extent and you will be a part of this family, where loyalty and honor is priceless. If you do decide to be a part of this and you play, lie or kick disloyalty in any way, you might as well go ahead and grab ya' gun and kill yourself now, or you can take that chance with playing with us and we can kill you and everything you've ever loved, including your pet fish. Nothing, and I mean nothing, is more important or bigger than this family. So, what's it gonna be? Choosing an answer is like flipping a coin. You never know what will happen, but you have to live with that decision forever. Let's be smart." He was starting to feel the demon talk through him.

Tay remained silent for a few seconds and held his hand out towards Ghost.

"Smart man."

Trouble and Woodie thought for a second and followed the same path Tay did, shaking hands with Ghost

Whether they knew it or not, if they didn't accept Ghost's hand or denied the proposition, they were going to be executed immediately in the Round Table room.

After Ghost finished giving his speech, D-Lo pulled him into the corner of the room. "Are you sure about this?

We don't even know these niggas. They could be rats," D-Lo said looking over Ghost shoulder.

"They ain't rats, bruh. They just need a little jump off to pipe up. They have no resources, but their loyalty towards each other is hundred. Now we gotta see if they can be loyal to anything else. Its chess, not checkers."

D-Lo shook his head, knowing what his brother had in mind.

Walking back to the table, Ghost looked at all three of them with a slick smile." I have a mission a piece for you all to begin with. Remember loyalty is the key, and betrayal equals death."

When Ghost left the room to take care of Tiffany's needs, D-Lo called for Tay to follow him as the rest of the crew stayed put. D-Lo walked outside, hopped in the car and began to break the mission down.

Chris Green

CHAPTER 8

"His name is Heavy, he's a known drug dealer and he supposedly traffics weight from Arizona to Cali. Heavy has been getting a little greedy and scratching at turf that's not his. Ghost doesn't like that very much."

"So, what do you want me to do, whack 'em?" Tay asked, looking over at D-Lo.

"That's up to you." D-Lo pointed at the Tec-9 laying on the backseat.

When they pulled up to Heavy's territory in the lower Beverly Hills area, Heavy sat inside the McDonald's parking lot in his green suburban on 26's, talking on the phone.

"You want me to do this right here?" Tay asked a little paranoid.

D-Lo looked over with a blank expression and shrugged.

Tay looked at the busy street and took a deep breath. "Fuck it." Grabbing the Tec, Tay exited the car and walked calmly across the street to the Mc Donald's. Heavy was so distracted that he never saw him creep up on the side of his truck. "What's hannin?" Tay said, putting the barrel of the gun inside the window.

As Heavy turned around, the first shot struck him in the neck. Falling to the floor, Tay released the Tec, spraying his body as the cars swerved to the right, speeding out of the driveway. After seeing his body slumped, he calmly walked back across the street to D-Lo's car and jumped in. D-Lo smiled as he crank up the car and left the scene.

As Suave and Woodie pulled into the apartment complex, a group of men were huddled in a circle, shooting dice and smoking weed. Certain dude's women accompanied them as they waited their turn to shoot next.

"You see the slim dude right there with the white polo shirt on?" Suave asked.

"Yeah," Woodie replied, looking at the tall man.

"Go 'head and take care of that nigga," Suave ordered. He fired up a Newport short, blowing out a cloud of smoke. "What about all the other people?"

Suave dumped his ashes out the window as he looked at Woodie. "What about 'em?"

Woodie shrugged as he got out of the car with the Mac 10 cradled under his shirt. As he got closer, he pulled the semi from under his shirt and busted through the crowd.

Poc! Poc! Poc! Poc! Poc! Poc! Poc! Poc!

Five people were instantly killed as he sprayed the 70-round clip angrily. As the bodies collapsed with the pavement, Woodie walked over to his target who was laying stiffly on the ground, trying to catch a breath of fresh air. He shot him between the eyes and watched him pass over to the afterlife. Then, he ran back to the car and got in. Suave said nothing as they swerved off, leaving over eight bodies of their collection laying in the street.

Trouble sat behind the wheel of Shadow's Charger as Tim occupied the passenger seat, smoking a blunt of Cali Kush.

"You know this family is kinda dangerous, right?" Tim asked, looking at Trouble seriously.

"Yeah, I kinda been understood and seen that."

Tim shook his head as he continued to hit his blunt. "Turn left on this next street."

As Trouble made the turn, Tim ordered him to pull over and let him out the car. He jumped out and got inside of the 96 Impala that sat directly on the side of the car.

Tim got inside of the car and crank it up. He then rolled the window down, looking at Trouble. "The person who you need to deal with is sitting at the end of the street."

"You ain't coming?" Trouble asked

"I wasn't instructed to come with you, only to tell you to complete the mission. Make it back to the house and you straight."

Trouble never experienced California before, because if he knew where he was, he would've turned around and did 150 miles per hour out of the section.

As Trouble pulled down the one-way street, he noticed the men that were located on tops of the buildings and houses. Some even had guns as they eyed his car recklessly. Keeping it moving down the one-way, Trouble rode past a group of bloods that mugged his car as he made his way to the end of the street. A man stood posted at the end of the corner, talking on his cell phone as Trouble pulled out his gun and rested it on his lap.

Pulling up to the end of the curve, the man turned around and walked to the car, sticking his head in the window. "Are you here for Ghost?"

"Yeah, I am," Trouble said, putting the pistol to the man's head and pulling the trigger.

Boc!

The 40 popped loudly, hitting the man square in the head.

The man's body jolted back out of the window, falling to the pavement. As Trouble swerved around, hitting a U-turn, guns were blazing, sending shot after shot burning through the car as he tried to exit the Concrete jungle.

Trouble ducked down, mashing the gas as the men appeared from behind the houses and rooftops. Everyone tried to turn the car into a shredded can as Trouble continued to duck down, feeling the glass slightly cutting the back of his neck. Speeding out of the projects, Trouble busted a right at the intersection to head back towards Ghost's Mansion.

As Ghost finished his session with Tiffany, he slid on his boxers. She was asleep, so he headed out of the room.

His new nanny Helena, a beautiful thick Spanish chick, played with the kids in the living room area. She winked at Ghost. He smiled and kept moving to Erica's room. Erica was laying on her stomach, sleeping as Ghost dropped his boxers and climbed behind her. He lifted her butt in the air, and before she could fully wake, Ghost was easing himself inside if her.

"Ahh! Baby," Erica moaned, cringing from his length.

He slowly spread Erica's ass as he watched his manhood fill her vagina. She arched her ass higher and buried her face inside her pillow as Ghost slid in a little harder, making her kitty fart.

"Damn, daddy," Erica cried out as she felt his huge dick bringing her closer to her climax.

After turning her over onto her back, Ghost slid back inside of Erica as he stuffed one of her breast in his mouth. He held her leg above his shoulder as he dug deep inside of her, feeling all her warmness.

"Ghost, baby, I'm sorry," Erica whispered in his ear as the tears ran down her face.

He kissed her lips, silencing her as he looked deeply into her eyes. Her cookie dripped profusely with her love cream as Ghost sped up, digging harder and releasing himself inside of her honey pot.

"I love you, and I will never turn my back on you or leave you behind," Ghost said as he kissed her lips and crawled off her.

After cleaning himself up, Ghost went and sat in his office as he thought about the destruction that was currently taking place. It was only a matter of time before they had to leave again and start over. He was prepared to make any move he had to so he could protect his children and his family. He always stayed ahead of the game. Even over his team. It was better that way because nothing beats the element of surprise.

Ghost picked up his phone and scrolled through his log until he reached the name Juicy. Dialing the number, he sat back in his chair and waited for an answer.

"Hi, Big Daddy," Sergeant Copeman said through the line.

"And how are you?" Ghost asked with a smirk on his face.

"Well, I'm fine now that I've talked to you. The city has been dying down since you left. Everybody has slowed down, paying attention to who's murdering who. I've been checking the data base from the FBI list. Even though they're investigating you, they don't physically have a warrant for your arrest, baby."

Ghost nodded his head in approval as he listened to her speak. "Listen, Ashley, I need your help. Do you think you can transfer funds to a private account?"

"Of course, I can, Papi. It's as easy as setting up a bank account. I can talk to my lawyers. He can set you up an account to the Virgin Islands, Cuba, or even Europe. He can liquidate all your valuables and transfer all your money to the account in less than 24 hours."

"Cool, and what do I owe you for doing this for me?"

"Hmmm, well you can always sneak down here to Atlanta and give me a little of that dinosaur tail, Mister." Ashley said in a seductive tone.

Ghost burst out laughing from her comment though he actually thought of the idea. "Is that all?"

Ashley remained quiet for a minute before she spoke. "You can bring me with you. I promise I won't be in the way. I'll find my own little place somewhere close to you and just relax. I mean as long as I'm a little close to you, I'll be okay. I'm just ready to be done with all this and just live my life."

Ghost pondered a minute on her request, thinking of how she actually could benefit him. "Okay."

Her heart skipped a beat after she heard his reply.

"Ghost, are you serious?" Ashley said with her stomach feeling as if butterflies were moving inside her.

"Of course, I am. That way. when I'm feeling a little freaky at night. I can slide through there and get in between that juicy you got between your legs."

"Shut up, with yo' crazy ass." She giggled, thinking of the possibility.

"Naw, I'm serious though, ma. You're coming with us. To be honest, I really need you. As soon as I get everything together, I'll call you."

"Alright, daddy." Ashley cheesed as she hung up the phone.

As Ghost continued to sit back in the office, getting ready to piece together their next getaway, D-Lo and Tay were the first two that walked through the door.

Suave and Woodie were second, coming in five minutes later. As the men sat in silence, Tim walked through the door.

"Did he make it?" Ghost asked, looking at him skeptically.

"I don't think so, Don," Tim said, taking a seat.

After five more minutes of waiting, Trouble came limping through the room as he looked at Ghost with a wicked smile. He walked around the table, sat down, pulled out his chair, and took a seat.

As Ghost looked at them all, a tiny smile crept on his face. "Welcome to The Black Team!" Ghost stood up as he pulled the golden key out of his pocket. "There's a trunk in my car that contains one hundred kilos of coke. D-Lo will give you all half of that. You already have a spot, weapons and access to any finances you need. When we have a mission for you all to complete, you will be notified with all details. Besides that, welcome to the La Familia."

As Ghost and the team embraced everyone in a brotherly hug, he grabbed Suave and whispered into his ear, "Keep your eye on him. If he even looks like he finna make a mistake, kill 'em." Ghost smiled, looking at Trouble out the corner of his eye.

Suave nodded, understanding as he walked off.

"Well fellas, everything is already in place for y'all. Y'all have the keys, you know where the spot at, let's get this money."

As everyone began to pile out the room, D-Lo stayed back with Ghost as Shadow walked in.

"I don't like none of those fat pussies out there. Are you even sure about these dudes?" Shadow asked. He disliked the idea of bringing complete strangers into their mix.

"Just chill, Shad, everything is a chess move. They won't be around long." Ghost chuckled at his best friend. While the three sat in the Round Table room they discussed the future plans for the team.

"I don't want any of us touching any more drugs. No killing unless absolutely necessary, and no one is to go anywhere without someone watching at all times."

"Say less," D-Lo said, standing up.

Suave walked back through the doors before Ghost could finish his conversation. "We got a problem," he said.

When he left again, Ghost, Shadow, and D-Lo made their way to the living room. Ghost went and looked out of the window. The swimming pool cleaners van was parked in the same exact spot it was last time. "So, these are the two y'all were telling me about?" Ghost asked as he continued to look out of the blinds.

"Yeah, that's them," D-Lo replied, standing at the other window next to Ghost.

"Cool. Strap up. We gone follow 'em."

As hours passed along and the van saw no movement coming from the house, he agents started the van and pulled off. Getting to the end of the street, the black Impala pulled out of the last parking lot and started to trail the van. After five minutes down the road, the Impala made a left turn as the van continued straight.

The two agents pulled into their safe house headquarters and exited the van.

"I guess we will have a little more luck tomorrow. Director Farmer only wants us to call in if we see him or Agent Harper," Agent Ross said as they entered the house.

Walking inside of the safe house, Agent Ross secured the door then walked down the hallway towards the living room.

"Gentlemen, gentlemen," Ghost said, scaring them half way to death. "We've been waiting over an hour and a half for you bitches to get home. I guess now you can explain the purpose of you sniffing around my house the past two weeks." Ghost looked at his watch.

The Black Team kept their guns aimed on the agents as the two men scrambled over their words.

"Kill em," Ghost pointed as he stood out of the chair. "You gentlemen have a good day." As Ghost walked past the agents, you could smell the shit that was starting to rise out of their pants.

Leaving out of the parking lot, Pablo's name flashed across the screen of Ghost's cell phone. "Hola, my friend." Ghost answered the phone, pulling out in the street.

"Ghost, amigo. I'm in need of your assistance at this time. Can we just say I have a little difficulty on my hands?"

"I'm on my way." He responded, hanging up

As Ghost made a U-turn to Pablo's house, he texted Tay's phone with the word BURN. Two minutes later, Tay texted back, "Already."

It was exactly twenty-five minutes later when Ghost arrived at Pablo's street. Pulling up to his yard, Sánchez buzzed the gate, letting him inside. Pablo met him at the front door, greeting him with a sincere, family hug and began to explain the issue.

"The man who is sitting in my living room is the lieutenant of the Russian Mafia. A couple months back he killed his boss and went renegade. He wants the forty-three percent of the coke deal that I was giving his head leader. I was his boss' connect. Fifteen million dollars is the debt that hasn't been payed because of his actions and stupidity. Now he's expecting to excuse this debt as if it never existed and do business."

Ghost silenced Pablo, holding his hand out for him to lead the way. As Pablo walked back into the living area, Frank Kelshekzi sat with his legs crossed, smoking a cigar with his three henchmen behind him.

Ghost stood behind Pablo as he took a seat. Before he could speak, Ghost interfered by grabbing his shoulder. "Hi. Frank, is it?" Ghost asked, stepping around Pablo to shake the man's hand.

"And might I ask who the fuck you are, my friend?" Frank asked in his strong Russian accent.

"Who I am isn't important, but the fifteen million dollars your organization owes Pablo is."

"Business with me is fresh like newborn baby. And unfortunately, I can't change diapers, my friend," Frank stated as his henchman laughed.

Ghost smiled. Looking at his cell phone, he hit the end button, then stuffed it back inside his pocket to look at the man in front of him. "I consider Pablo a father to me. Your disrespect has not only offended me and him, but everything we stand for. You have five minutes to transfer that money to Pablo, or I'm afraid there won't be any talking or anything left to discuss."

Frank stood up out of his seat to move closer to Ghost. "Is that a threat, my friend?"

"No, sir, it's a choice."

Frank smiled as he blew the cigar smoke in Ghost's face. "My family were real mean people. We were raised killing and slaughtering monkeys like you. In my country, for your disrespect, we would gang rape your mother, addict her to heroine, and months later slit her throat, throwing her in the fucking ocean for the sharks to finish her. Now you have two days to have my family a nice supply of a hundred and fifty kilos of cocaine, or I will kill you, him and anyone who resembles you ugly peasants. You understand me, nigga?" Frank asked, taking off his hat.

"Capeesh," Ghost replied with slanted eyes.

As they exited Pablo's house, Frank and his men retreated to their car and got in. After cranking the car, Frank rolled his window down to speak.

"And just for the record—" were the last words Frank could speak before the car blew up into a thousand pieces, killing all four men instantly.

Shadow sat on the hood of the black Impala with his black Ray Ban's on as he looked at the sparks fly. Pablo's face was stuck as he wondered who he really gotten himself involved with.

Ghost turned around and hugged Pablo. "You go ahead inside and get some rest. I will get someone to clean this up."

Pablo nodded, still amazed as his henchmen took him inside and locked the door.

Ghost watched the flames eviscerate the car. He walked across the driveway to Shadow. "Have someone come clean this up. Make it extra quick. We have to be at the club tonight."

Shadow shook his head and got on his iPhone as Ghost jumped in his car and pulled off.

Chris Green

CHAPTER 9

The club's atmosphere was ecstatic tonight. Lots of cash was being thrown and the girls looked better than ever. Sheika was the newest member of the girls. A 6-foot butter cookie skinned amazon with mad booty and a top 10 magazine face.

Suave and Tay ran security at the front of the club as Shadow, Trouble and Woodie were spread out around the floor. As Ghost sat in his office counting the money, Tiffany and Erica sat on the couch next to each other in matching but different color Versace dresses. Their hair and their nails were done to the T as they sat quietly on the couch, looking out of the 2-way window. D-Lo stood by the door with his gun in his hand as he watched the dance floor.

Pulling up to the club was a red Chevy on 24's that blared Lil' Wayne's *Hollyweezy* through the speakers as it found a spot and parked.

Bullshit stepped out of the car with his nose tooted from all the good cocaine he was snorting all day. He dressed in all red and a Chicago Bulls snapback. Shooter stepped out of the passenger side, adjusting his pistol on his waist. Then, they headed towards the entrance.

"Whoa, my nigga. Where the fuck y'all think y'all going. No gang banging ass niggas allowed," Suave said, putting his hand on Bullshit's chest.

Bullshit looked at Suave's hand and slapped it down. "Nigga, who the fuck you think you be? I'm paying like everybody else. I should be able to get in this bitch when I want to."

Suave grabbed the bridge of his nose to try and relax himself. "Look, you two fuck niggas better go and find a house party to crash, or it's gone get way bloodier than you two bitches think you are."

As Bullshit indulged in the argument, it began to grow. The whole team made their way from the dance floor and office to the outside with Suave and Tay.

"What seems to be the problem?" Ghost asked, stepping to the front with the Team on his heels.

When Bullshit laid eyes on Ghost, he reached for his pistol. Before he could lift his hand, the Black Team, along with D-Lo, Suave, and Shadow, had their guns beaming down on Shooter and him.

"Nice to meet you, Sir," Ghost said with a smile, holding his hand out.

"Naw, fuck you, blood. You know who the fuck I am?" Bullshit spat with his pistol pointed at him.

The crowd that waited to get in the club stood silently against the walls as the men stared each other down.

"I'm afraid I don't recall knowing you at all." Ghost chuckled, pulling out a cigarette to light it.

"Yeah, right. Same way you don't know my little bro Devon you just killed. Or what about Twan back in Atlanta, huh?" Bullshit shouted, trying to psych himself out.

Ghost looked up at the sky as if he was trying to find an answer or as if he was trying to remember. "Naw, I guess I don't."

"Oh, trust, you'll be able to remember soon. I know exactly who you are, Chance."

Shooter sat in silence as he stared at Ghost and D-Lo motionless.

Ghost looked at D-Lo, hearing the man call his name. "How about we take a rain check on this 'do I know you' shit. Let me finish running my business and we can handle all this when we see each other, blood." Ghost said with a smirk on his face.

Bullshit and Shooter held eye contact as they walked back to the car and climbed in. The tensions were high in the air as they crank the music up, swerving off.

"Their gonna be a problem," D-Lo said as he and Ghost watched the car speed away.

"Find out where they are, and kill 'em. Let's resume our night, people," Ghost said, grabbing Tiffany and Erica to lead them back inside the club.

It was more than a week that passed before Tim and J.L. got out of the hospital. Ghost pulled up to the house in a new Benz CL class 600. As Ghost got out, he helped Tim out the backseat as D-Lo and the Black Team pulled up right behind them with J.L. in the passenger. As the Dons made their way into the crib, Ghost thought to himself that the team was officially back.

"Say, baby, me and Bernard are gonna go out for a ride and pick up a few things, and get a little breather," Erica said, giving Ghost a hug.

"Okay, baby, take one of the fellas to ride with you," he replied, sipping his drink.

"It's okay. Were only gonna be out a few minutes, and we're coming right back."

"Are you sure?"

"I'm positive, lovebug."

"Naw, I'll ride with her. I need to see if I can find me a new pair of shoes anyway, baby." Tiffany said, grabbing her Chanel bag.

Ghost's face turned into a wide smirk. "You have over sixty pairs of shoes that you don't even wear, Tiff."

"There's never enough, baby." Tiffany pecked his lips before walking off.

Ghost shook his head as the girls made their way out the door. "To da Mobb!" He yelled to his brothers as they all raised their hands in the air.

As Erica and Tiffany rode in silence down the street, Tiffany broke the bubble as she looked over at her.

"So, let's get something straight. It can be no way we're staying in the same house and we're not getting along. You obviously don't want to share Ghost and neither do I, but it seems like he loves both of us and our children. So, whether you like it or not, were family, Erica," Tiffany said

"First of all, I never had a problem with you. I can honestly say I didn't like what was going on at first, but I've learned to understand that Ghost is crazy and he's going to get what he wants regardless." Erica replied as she pulled into the shopping area and found a place to park. As she cut the car off, her eyes shifted over at Tiffany. "Listen, I'm not dumb. I know you and Ghost have sex, but does he really make love to you like you're his only woman?"

"Of course, he does. But I feel like he's making love to someone else."

Erica thought for a minute before she spoke. "Look, Tiffany, I know that Ghost loves you, and soon I know our love will be just as strong for one another. I just know that we both want to make him happy and I know he will be happy if me and you put our difficulties to the side and love each other."

Tiffany licked her lips, looking at Erica. "Can I ask you a question?"

"Sure."

"How come you've never came in the room and got in the bed with me and Ghost?"

She stumbled over her words from the question Tiffany brought upon her. "I mean... I don't know I guess. I just... ya' know, kinda didn't know how to." Erica was trying to find the right words to spit out.

Tiffany reached over, grabbed Erica's face, and stuck her tongue in her mouth. Erica's heart fluttered, wanting to stop Tiffany, but it felt so right. As she kissed Erica, her hand slid down to her warm pussy as she rubbed it lightly.

"You don't have to be scared of me. You're always welcome in our bedroom."

Erica backed away as she felt herself getting aroused. "Umm, Tiffany what are you doing? Bernard is in the back seat."

Tiffany raised off of Erica and squinted her green eyes sexily. Looking down at her pussy print, she smirked slightly. "Maybe you'll think about it and I'll get to taste a little of that caramel."

"Come on, let's go shopping," Erica said nervously as she got out of the car, readjusting her wet panties.

After grabbing Bernard, the girls made their way towards the stores.

Across town, Bullshit sat in his car as he spoke to Co-Co's sister on the phone. "So, do you think you can set this motherfucker up or what?" Bullshit spoke roughly through the phone.

"I don't know, Bull. I can't do anything but try my best. All I have to do is get him to the hotel room, right?" Tyra asked, scared from the whole idea.

"I don't give a fuck if you gotta suck the skin off that nigga's dick, don't let him go nowhere."

"I don't know about this, Bullshit. What if somebody gets hurt?"

"Bitch, this is a robbery! Nobody's gonna get hurt, Tyra. Either you can do this or we can tell Co-Co how you and your friends would steal her money and come fuck and suck me behind her back."

"You don't have to do all of that, Ralph, I'm going to do it."

"Bitch, don't call me that. Just make sure you're at the club Thursday night." Bullshit hung up in her face. He threw the phone in the other seat as he thought in his own world. He never wanted to kill somebody as bad as he wanted to kill Ghost. The vibration of his phone snapped him out of his daze as he looked at the name that flashed across the screen. "Yes, sir?"

"Why isn't he finished yet? I told you this was a delicate situation for me. He's supposed to be in a box, six feet under. What part of that isn't registering in your brain?"

"I'm trying, Pa, he's fucking smart. Every time—"

"Quiet!" the man said, cutting Bullshit off. "In the next month, this abomination better be dead. Or, I can just send someone to do it myself and also to do you. Is that understood?"

"Yes, sir."

"I love you son, but I refuse to have any weakness in this family."

"I understand, Pa," Bullshit said more in his Spanish accent before he hung up the phone.

CHAPTER 10

Walking through the mall, Tiffany held Bernard as Erica carried the shopping bags. After running through mostly all the high-end designer stores, the girls finished their shopping rampage and headed to the car. After throwing the bags in the trunk, the girls strapped the baby in the seat and pulled off.

After cruising down the road for about five minutes, a Los Angeles police cruiser blue lighted Erica, getting directly behind her.

"Fuck," she mumbled, slowing the car down a little, looking over at Tiffany. "I don't think I should stop."

"Ugh, ya' think? You're a federal agent on the run with a criminal mastermind," Tiffany told her.

"But what about Bernard?"

"Just stop. Maybe it's a regular routine pullover."

"And what if it's not?" Erica asked, feeling the worst about to occur.

Tiffany shrugged and pulled out her baby glocc. "Then we'll have to make it home the best way possible."

As Erica slowed the car down, the police officer came to a halt at the rear of her bumper. Stepping out, the officer adjusted his hat and walked towards the driver's side door. Walking up, the officer tapped on the window.

"Hi, officer, is there a problem?" Erica asked, easing the window down with a smile on her face.

"You were doing seventy-five in a fifty. Can I see your license and registration?" The officer asked, bending down in the window of the car.

"Um, okay." Erica grabbed the information it and handed it over to the officer.

After the officer told the girls to sit still, he walked to his car and began to enter her information into the database.

"Listen, if he says the wrong thing, it's no looking back." Erica whispered, looking at Tiffany.

"Bitch, I live for this. You better make sure you're ready."

As Erica gripped the steering wheel nervously, the officer walked back over towards the car.

"Ma'am, your license has been suspended by the government and there's a federal warrant out on your name. Do you happen to know about that?"

"No, sir, I've never been in trouble my whole life," Erica responded, feeling her heart beat a little harder.

The officer grabbed his walkie talkie to call for backup. "Ma'am, I'm gonna have to ask you to step out of the car." The officer said with his hand on his gun.

Tiffany looked at Erica and nodded. Erica closed her eyes and took a deep breath. "I'm sorry, sir, I can't do that."

"Ma'am, that's a direct order. Step out of the car." The officer reached for the door handle.

Off instinct, Tiffany leaned across Erica's lap, shooting the officer in the jaw.

Boc!

"Go!" she screamed, seeing the man hit the ground.

Erica mashed the pedal, making the car skate off out of control. Bernard screamed to the top of his lungs as Erica revved the car up to 100 miles per hour down the strip.

"Call Ghost!" Erica screamed.

As Tiffany stumbled and fidgeted, she got a hold of her phone and dialed his number.

"Hello?" Ghost answered with a blunt in between his lips.

"Baby, we have a problem!" Tiffany yelled through the phone.

"What's wrong?" He listened and quieted the boys.

"We got pulled over and the officer tried to arrest Erica."

"So, what the fuck happened?"

"I shot him, bae," Tiffany said, feeling she fucked up.

"You did what? Where the fuck is my child, Tiffany?"

"He's in the backseat."

Before Tiffany could say another word, two cop cars pulled from the intersecting street as the pursuit began.

"They're behind us, Ghost."

"Fuck," Ghost said, gripping the phone so tight that he almost crushed it. "Load up!" He yelled to the team as they all moved around quickly. "Tiffany?"

"Yes?"

"Listen to me, baby, I need you and Erica to make it to the bridge that sits two blocks down from the house."

"And then what Ghost?"

"Then I want you to speed as fast as you can to Erica's house. No stopping. I'll be on the bridge waiting."

The team ran outside to get in their cars.

"Okay, were coming!" she shouted, hanging up the phone.

Tiffany gave Erica the instructions Ghost gave her to follow as the police yelled *"pull over"* through their megaphones.

"Don't stop!"

"I'm not going to stop, I'm trying to get the fuck away," Erica screamed, smashing off to the right of the road.

Tiffany held Bernard's car seat when Erica made the wide turn.

Erica floored the car down the street until she came up towards the next street where the bridge rested. Making the turn, the tire slammed against the curve, making her slide as she fought to keep the car in control. She ran over the next curve, knocking down the stop sign as she swerved through the grass.

"We're almost there! The bridge is up ahead!" Tiffany screamed as Erica got control of the car and hit the gas harder.

The two cop cars could barely keep up with the SRT engine that was inside of her Challenger. She reached the front of the bridge doing 130 miles per hour.

Ghost and the team were parked, sitting on top of the trunk and cars when they spotted Erica approaching.

"That's Ghost right there, I see him. I see him." Erica focused in, approaching at a fast pace. As she flew past them the team blocked the bridge off.

Ghost smiled, looking at the approaching cars. "Kill 'em," he said calmly.

"What the fuck?" The officer said, witnessing the men blocking the street off. Before they could stop or U-turn, the boys' guns were blazing like the 4th of July.

Bocccc! Boc! Boc! Boc! Boc! Boc! Bocccc!

Ghost sat on the hood of the car as he watched his brothers Swiss Cheese both the police cruisers.

The first eight bullets struck the officer in one car, making him flip six times before he crashed through the fence off the bridge. After the second officer hit the wall, he crawled towards the backseat as the bullets rained through the thin cruiser. The team progressed, still firing their weapons as the officer laid in the backseat, ducking from being struck.

D-Lo jumped on top of the windshield, sending shots through the glass, striking the him in the side. Opening the back door of the car, Woodie snatched the officer out by his feet, making his head crash against the pavement. The officer held on to his side as the team surrounded him.

Ghost walked over and broke the circle as he stared at the officer.

"Just do it," the officer said, looking into Ghost's evil eyes.

"Okay," Woodie agreed, putting the gun in his face.

"Whoa," Ghost stopped him, pushing the gun down. "I think I got a better plan for Mr. Oink here. Pick his ass up."

As the officer was picked up off the ground, Shadow looked over at Ghost. "What the hell are you doing?"

"Take 'em to the car," Ghost ordered the team. He smiled as he looked back at Shadow. "We're going to keep him. Let's just say as a little deposit."

"Are you sure about this, Ghost?"

"I'm positive."

Hearing the sirens, Ghost and Shadow ran back to the car and sped off as his team left another tragedy for California to clean up.

After pulling up to Erica's driveway, Ghost and Shadow parked and made their way into the house.

Erica and Tiffany were sitting on the couch when she saw a picture of her car pop up on the news. Tiffany turned up the volume as the team looked on in silence.

"It's still unclear what happened today in the Beverly Hills area. These suspects are labeled to be highly dangerous after an officer was shot in the face, near the lower part of his jaw. The camera from the side of a building caught this blurry picture of the license plate belonging to the dark blue Dodge Challenger. Miles away was a tragic accident, or homicide, of the other authority officers involved. One officer was pronounced dead on the scene and the whereabouts of Detective Jameson are still unknown. If you have any information on the car in this picture, please call the Crime Stoppers Hotline."

Erica sat back in shock, looking at the blurry picture the camera caught of her swerving away from the scene.

"Welcome to the family, baby," Ghost said, smooching her cheeks with a kiss before walking off.

Erica sat spaced out as she tried to wrap her mind around being a wanted criminal now.

"It's okay, sis," D-Lo said, putting his hand on her shoulder. "You family, and family always have each other's back."

Erica looked up at D-Lo and nodded.

"How about we pay Mr. Piggy a visit?" Ghost suggested as he walked back into the living room.

As they made their way out of the room and headed to the basement, Ghost pulled out his glocc 40 and walked in, heading down the steps.

The officer sat in the chair unconscious from all the blood he'd recently lost. He was tied down to the chair as his feet sat propped up on a cylinder block of concrete. The squad spread around the room as Ghost walked in front of the officer, tapping the side of his leg with the gun.

He took the small cup he had in his hand and splashed the officer with the urine. Officer Jameson began to cough and spit vigorously as the stench and taste polluted his senses. "What the fuck? Where the fuck am I?" he asked as he looked at the seven men and two women that stood in front of him. "Who are you people?" He struggled to get free from the restraints.

"Calm down," Ghost said as he held the officers shoulder.

The officer continued to buck and was struck with a hard-right hand.

"I need your help with something. As you can see, we hate officers. You tried to arrest my baby's mother today and that kind of turned out a little bad on you guys' end. So, I need you to help direct a little traffic for your friends."

"You all are gonna be under the jail when my boys find you. I'll make sure you can at least eat the vegetables off the tray while your roommate is trying to fuck your asshole off your body in Alcatraz prison, motherfucker."

"Oh yeah?"

"That's right," he said, looking at Ghost with an arrogant stare.

"Well how about I just go and see Lily? I know she's at school right now. I can pay a couple of junkies to rape her and kill her. Or what about your wife Vivian? She wouldn't even know what hit her until my brother blows her brains out all over her hair products. Background checks are really easy when you gotta smart laptop and a criminal." Ghost already had the scoop on the officer.

"You stay away from my family, you filthy, pussy scumbag. Whatever we have going on doesn't have anything to do with my wife and daughter, coward."

Ghost chuckled. "I'll make sure your wife sucks my dick really good and slow. And when I explode in her mouth, a bullet will explode through her head. Shadow, convince this bitch that he's a pussy and not me." Ghost said, sitting down.

"Say no more." Shadow picked up the scissor grip pliers and cut three of the officer's fingers off.

"Arrrgggghhhhhh, aahhhh, fuckkkkkk!" The officer's voice turned into more of a womanly scream as his fingers hit the ground.

Shadow crank up the blow torch and burned his fingers to stop the blood from pouring. Cutting the torch off, he sat back as the officer began to shit his pants and howl in pain.

He dropped his head in a defeated manner as he mumbled, "Fuck you," in an incoherent tone.

Ghost shook his head. "Try his little friend inside his pants, Shadow."

Shadow shook his head as he tried to snatch the man's pants off.

"Okay, okay, what do you want me to do?" the officer asked with his eyes as big as dinner plates.

"I want you to do whatever the fuck we tell you to do, and then you and your family are free to go."

"Why are you doing this?" the officer asked, trying to shake the dizziness away as he looked into Ghost's eyes.

"Clean him up," Ghost said, smiling. While he was sitting in the fold out chair, his cell phone rang. "Whoa?"

The loud bang of the gunshot confused Ghost as the static and crackling maneuvered through his ears.

"What's popping, blood?" Bullshit asked through the phone before hanging up.

Ghost sat in silence as he pondered on what had just happened.

"Whoa, who the fuck was that, bruh?" D-Lo asked, watching his brother stuck in motion.

"Call Chucc," Ghost said. He stood as still and as numb as a mannequin.

D-Lo rushed in front of his brother, looking in his face. "Bruh, wassup?" he panicked, grabbing his shoulder.

"Bullshit just called me from Hotboy's phone," Ghost said, stunned.

D-Lo snatched his phone out his pocket to dial Chucc's phone number.

"What's good bro?" Chucc answered on the third ring in a relaxed tone.

"Whoa, where are you, bro? Are you around Hotboy?"

"Naw. Bro, I'm out here at this little strip club joint on the East. Hotboy's at the spot."

"Get over there now!" D-Lo screamed through the phone.

"Alright man, I'm leaving right now," Chucc said, hearing the urgency in his brother's voice.

D-Lo hung up the phone looking at his brother. "Do you want me to grab the Black Team and head out that way?"

"I want to know where Hotboy is," Ghost replied.

D-Lo nodded and just decided to wait for the call.

As the team stood in the basement in quietness. the vibration from the phone broke the silence. Everyone looked around, checking their phones. Seeing that it wasn't theirs, they realized the officer's eyes were filled with nervousness as his pocket sounded off louder and harder. Ghost turned his head, looking in the officer's direction. Walking towards him, he bent down, making the man tense up.

Hearing the vibration again, Ghost dug in the man's back pocket and removed a thin Verizon touchscreen. When Ghost looked at the phone, the name that sat on the front screen made his heart skip a beat. He looked in the officer's eyes as they began to fill with fear. Ghost clicked the button and answered the line as the room listened to the other side.

"Yo', Phil. Where the fuck are you? Pa wants this motherfucker dead immediately. Hello?" Bullshit said, speaking through the phone.

The team looked bewildered hearing the voice that boomed through the line.

Ghost threw the phone across the room wear it crumbled to pieces when hitting the wall. Then, he put his gun to the center of the officer's head. "You got five seconds to tell me what the fuck is going on, or I'ma spatter yo' fucking brains on the ceiling."

The officer's eyes bulged as he realized everyone's faces in the room turned from confused to sinister. Ghost pointed his gun at the officer's thigh and blew a hole through it.

Boc!

Erica covered her ears when hearing the man yell loud enough to scare her.

"I said talk, motherfucker!" Ghost screamed, putting the gun up to the man's eye.

"Okayyy! Wait! Wait!" The officer shouted, sweating bullets as the piss began to run down his leg. "Please, Ghost, you wouldn't understand. Just give me time to tell you." The man said, feeling his thigh burn like an open fire.

"How the fuck do you know my name? Start fucking talking." He gritted, pressing the gun against his eye harder.

"The man I work for, he's the reason all these things have been happening to you."

"I think you need to be more specific about what the fuck is going on," D-Lo said as his phone began to ring. "Whoa," D-Lo spoke, putting the phone on speaker.

"Bro, I'm here," Chucc said in a defeated tone.

"Where is Hotboy?" Ghost asked, grabbing the phone.

"He's lying in the middle of the floor in front of me. It's bad, bro."

Ghost's heart tightened as he heard the fate of his friend. He cut his eyes back at the officer. "Give me a name," he demanded with his look turning from crazy to psychopath.

The officer looked at Ghost's face and knew he was prepared to kill him. "His name is Jesus Ramirez."

Ghost looked back at Shadow and D-Lo who were just as confused as he was. "Who the fuck is he?"

The officer looked Ghost in the eyes and told him what he wanted to hear. "I've worked for him almost twenty years. He's not going to stop until you're dead, Ghost. He's not going to forgive you.

"I said who the fuck is he?"

The officer swallowed his spit before he responded. "He's your grandfather."

Everyone's face in the room went stale besides D-Lo's.

Ghost chuckled as a wicked smile stained his face. "Nice knowin' ya'." He then put the pistol to the officer's head.

"I knew your father," the officer screamed, seeing his finger grip the trigger harder. "You were no older than three years old, Chance. Your father was a very dangerous man," Officer Jameson continued, staring at D-Lo and Ghost. "He made no exceptions for anyone and had an explosive temper. Your father was murdered by your grandfather after he stole fifty million dollars from his family-owned business."

Ghost held the guns to the man's head as he listened to him speak.

"Your grandfather is one of the richest Spanish cocaine dealers in America. Do you think it's a coincidence that we pulled your little girlfriend over today? Or what about your distribution house that was riddled with bullets? No! It's not a coincidence. Your father betrayed his familia. He defiled your granddad's trust, so Jesus put a price on his head, making him flee from California. Look at you and your brother. Does it make any sense to you? What about the long hair that your brother has or the curly hair on your head? What about the fluent Spanish your mother used to speak when you were younger?"

Ghost listened as the officer dispersed info only a close person to his family would know.

"Your father's name is Michael Gunna Ramirez. He was one of the youngest notorious killers in California, to Atlanta and Louisiana. Your father stole the fifty million and tried to run off to Atlanta to start a new life with his own family. Except for one thing," Officer Jameson said, breathing erratically.

"What's that, motherfucker?" Ghost asked, feeling his heart turn blacker by the second.

"His heart couldn't let him leave his third child behind."

D-Lo and Ghost's eyes found each other as they listened and felt the truth in the man's voice. The room stayed in silence as the man continued.

"Your father cheated on your mother on a normal basis. His infidelity led to a child by a woman named Elaine Williams."

Ghost's heart began to race as he heard the name come from the Detective's mouth.

"Whoa, hold up. Did you say Elaine Williams?" Shadow asked as he stood.

The officer smiled as he looked at Ghost and nodded.

"So, your telling me Twan was my fucking brother?" Ghost asked in total confusion.

"Yes, you killed your own brother. Not only that, but you've killed multiple people out of your own family. Your grandfather despises you and he wants your head for killing his third grandson. You're gonna die, Ghost," the officer said, letting the truth free.

"D-Lo, do you know anything about this?"

"I can't remember, lil' bro. This shit is too much. I haven't remembered mama saying anything about our grandfather since we were young."

"I wonder why." The officer said, starting to breathe a little slower.

"Where the fuck can I find him?" Ghost asked aggressively.

The officer chuckled as he stared at the gun. "You can't find him 'cause you're already dead."

"Okay, well make sure you tell him I'm coming for his ass too." Ghost shot the officer between the eyes.

Boc!

As the officer's body slumped in the chair, Ghost turned around and looked at everybody.

"Whoever these people are, find them, kill them, and let's get the fuck out of California." Ghost then headed back upstairs.

Chris Green

CHAPTER 11

Ghost walked swiftly through the back of the town homes' parking lot. After looking at his watch, he saw that it was 11:30PM. He moved quickly over to the end of the building and began to climb the metal water pipe that lead him to the second-floor balcony. After jumping over the rail, Ghost walked to the two porch doors to look inside. The TV played at an average volume and the light to the bathroom shined brightly. Ghost wiggled the door knob to the first door. It shook but it wouldn't open. Still watching his surroundings and observing the inside of the house, he tried the second door that opened with ease.

Sliding inside the darkness of the living room, Ghost eased the patio door closed and looked around the mediocre apartment. Heading towards the bedroom, Ghost noticed that the shower was running and the door was slightly ajar. The steam from the bathroom hung thick in the air as Ghost walked towards the door and slowly pushed it open. He walked over to the shower and pulled the curtain open.

Co-Co bathed under the hot water. "Ghost, what the fuck?" she yelled, covering herself.

"Bitch, shut up. It ain't like I ain't ever seen you naked. Get out the shower and meet me in the living room."

"Well, can you let me get a little privacy, nigga? How the fuck did you get in my house?"

Ghost looked at her perfectly shaven kitty and smiled. "Can I get a little privacy with that?" Ghost asked, rubbing his finger across her clit.

"Nope, nigga. Don't you got two bitches at home you can fuck?" She flexed, letting him get his feel on.

"Yeah, I do, but that don't mean I don't want this pussy." Ghost pulled out his dick.

Co-Co looked down at Ghost's member and she instantly became wet. She stepped out of the shower and led him to the living room couch. After she sat him down, she got on her knees and took him into her mouth. Both of her small hands twirled up and down Ghost's shaft as she sucked on the tip of his dick. She began to take long slurps as she forced as much as she could down her throat.

"Fuck!" Ghost moaned, grabbing the back of her head as she looked into his eyes. The slurping of her mouth turned Ghost on even more as he slapped her juicy, red ass that sat in the air.

"You taste so good, daddy." Co-Co said, licking the side of his rod.

"Damn, ma, you gotta slow down." He removed himself from her mouth and walked behind her.

Co-Co lifted her ass high in the air on all fours as she buried her face in the carpet.

He looked at her ass, rubbing it slowly as he went inside of her pink kitty.

"Oouuuu, shit," Co-Co moaned, feeling the monster slide inside of her slowly and hard.

Ghost caught his rhythm as her ass bounced widely against his shaft. He looked down as he watched himself enter her back and forth.

"Fuck this pussy, baby."

"I got you, ma," Ghost said as he pounded away in her soft, wetness. He continued to hold on to her ass cheeks as he exploded inside of her walls. "Shit," he swore as he pulled his dick out, rubbing it across her butt.

"Damn, daddy." Co-Co smiled, still bent over on the floor. "I want you to keep going."

"I got you, ma." Ghost pulled the baby glocc from his pocket and shot her once in the back of the head.

Standing up, he fixed his clothes and grabbed Co-Co's cellphone off the table. He began to scroll through her apps as to find the message box. Clicking on the first one, he read the message slowly.

Girl, where are you? I was about to come over. Bullshit looking for you. –Tyra

Ghost clicked the reply button and began to type his message. *I'm not at home. Meet me at E. 137th St. in L.A. and Bullshit ain't talking 'bout shit girl, lol!*

Ghost sat down on Co-Co's couch as he waited for a reply. Two minutes later the phone began to vibrate.

Lol. Alright, I'm on the way in one hour, but I think he's serious about setting this dude Ghost up.

He quickly smiled at the message and clicked the reply button. *We'll talk about that when I see you.* Ghost then pressed the send button.

He stood up, sliding the phone down in his pocket, and looked at Co-Co's naked body on the floor. He shook his head and began to smile. "Now that's just a good piece of ass gone to waste."

He left the same way he came in.

After he made his way back down the metal drains into the parking lot, he waved for Shadow to pull off as he hopped in Co-Co's car and headed out behind him. Ghost's phone rang in his pocket as he and Shadow pulled out of the area.

"Hello?"

"What the hell took you so long in there?" Shadow asked.

"We were talking." He grinned, lying quickly.

"Ghost you're fucking disgusting." Shadow laughed in his ear and hung up.

He couldn't help but to laugh as he put his phone back up and headed to his next destination.

CHAPTER 12

Chucc got out of his brand-new Charger and headed up the steps to Ghost's house. He rang the doorbell and he waited for an answer.

Tiffany answered the door after the third knock, looking at him like he was crazy. "Wassup? Ghost ain't here," Tiffany said with a frown.

"I got a text from him twenty minutes ago, saying pull up at the spot."

"Well. I guess you just gone have to come in and wait, 'cause he might not be back for a couple of hours." Tiffany let him in.

As she closed the door and began to walk off, Chucc noticed she didn't have any pants or underwear on. Licking his lips seductively, he couldn't help but to say something. "Damn, Ghost know you walking around the house like that?"

Tiffany stopped and looked at him with a crooked face. "I do whatever the fuck I want. I'm grown."

"Oh yeah. Why is it so dark in here? Ain't nobody here with you?"

"Why? You scared?" Tiffany asked, looking at him funny.

"Please, I ain't scared of a damn thing." Chucc replied arrogantly.

"Oh yeah? I bet you ain't man enough to touch Ghost's pussy." Tiffany spread her legs, showing her pretty lips.

She knew that Chucc craved for her. She saw it in his eyes numerous times, and he still never had the heart to say it.

"See, I knew it. You another pussy who's terrified of Ghost." She laughed softly, looking at Chucc who was frozen in place.

"Fuck Ghost. He ain't even a factor no more."

"And why is that? You must think you man enough to take his place. You think you ready for a spot like that?" Tiffany asked seductively.

"In a few days, Ghost won't have a spot after Bullshit gets a hold of him."

"So why you been rocking with Ghost and you know you working with his enemy?"

"I do whatever necessary to get to the top. But what about you? You sitting here half naked on the couch, trying to pick my brain. You must be trying to slide on my team and do this shit the right way." Chucc walked over to the couch and sat next to her.

"I'm down with whoever the realest."

"How about you let me show you how real I am?" Chucc replied, spreading her legs apart to put his hand at her sweet spot.

"I don't think you can handle or have none of this pussy, and this good," she blushed, watching him get on his knees in front of her.

"I'm better at showing." Chucc licked his tongue across her clit.

Tiffany leaned her head back in satisfaction as Chucc began to let his tongue explore her insides. "Mmmmm!" she moaned, grabbing the back of his head as he feasted on her pussy lips.

Chucc slid a finger back and forth in her tight spot as he massaged his thumb on her asshole.

"Shit," Tiffany said, feeling herself on the verge of cumming on his tongue.

Chucc began to taste her juices as she bust her nut directly on his lips. "This pussy so sweet, ma," Chucc said as he continued to suck on her pearl tongue.

He leaned his head up as he slid down his pants, removing his dick. He placed his hands on Tiffany's stomach and tried to enter her from the front.

"Hold up, daddy," Tiffany said, putting her hand on him. "I gotta taste that dick."

Tiffany stood up and unhooked her bra with her eyes on the gun that hung slightly from the waistline of his boxers. Chucc held on to his gun as she got on her knees, looking him in the eye. He leaned back in satisfaction as she shoved his member into her mouth. She sucked greedily back and forth as she massaged his scrotum.

"Damn, ma, keep doing that shit," Chucc said. He saw her deep throat him, come back up to the tip, and suck extra hard.

She did what she was told, deep throating him again. When she came back up to the head of his manhood, the blade in her hand came down, disconnecting his dick from his body.

"Ahhhhhhh! Fuckinnngg bitch!" Chucc screamed louder as he pulled his gun from his boxers.

Tiffany slapped the gun out of his hand and kicked him in the nuts, making him crash against the floor. She picked up the gun and stood over him. His eyes bulged in pain. He couldn't speak or breathe as the blood squirted through his fingers that held his private.

Tiffany giggled as she looked at Chucc's little wiener sitting on the floor. "You're a stupid little man. I told you that you couldn't handle this pussy and head, little boy."

"I'm gonna fucking kill you, bitch," Chucc said, feeling his energy drain from his body.

"Mmm hmm. That's the same thing my man wanted me to tell you, snake ass motherfucker." Tiffany mugged as she put two slugs into Chucc's heart.

Boc! Boc!

She moved with expertise as she wiped her fingerprints off the gun, slid it back inside the lining of his boxers, and retrieved her pants.

Pulling out her cell phone, she dialed Ghost's number.

"Hello?"

"It's done, baby."

"Good, go back over to Erica's," Ghost whispered through the phone.

"Okay, daddy," Tiffany replied, walking out of the house and locking the door behind her.

Tyra pulled in front of the house and parked her car next to Co-Co's. Stepping out, her phone vibrated with a message.

Come in girl, the door is unlocked.

Tyra looked at the weird house suspiciously as she walked up the steps. Opening the front door, she walked in and shut the door behind her. "Co-Co, where you at, bitch?" Tyra said, looking crazy in the deserted living room.

"Right here," Ghost said, making her shit out her heart as she turned around.

His right hand collided upon her chin before she was able to utter a scream. As she crashed to the floor unconsciously, Ghost grabbed her by her feet and drug her body into the nearest bedroom.

As she opened her eyes, the blurriness started to clear as she witnessed Shadow zip-tie her feet. The handcuffs that held her hands behind her back began to tighten as she tried to sit up.

"Whoa, hold on, sweetheart, you gone kill yourself before I get a chance to." Shadow said, making her scoot up against the wall.

Ghost posted against the wall with two thick brown bags in his hand as he stared in Tyra's eyes.

"Do you know who I am?" Ghost asked, feeling a little sorry for her.

"No! Where is my sister?"

"Co-Co's asleep right now. She might not wake up for the next few years." Ghost informed her with an evil smile.

"Who are you? Why do you have me here?" Tyra asked, trying to feel her wrist that were getting tighter in the handcuffs.

"Well sweetie, unfortunately, I killed the last victim and it's Shadow's turn to show off. So, you have to speak to him."

"Okay, listen here, cupcake. You got two bags right here." Shadow said, holding them both in the air. "Ghost is gonna ask you a few questions, and if you get it wrong, you gotta pick a bag. Now what's inside is the surprise. So, try not to get too many wrong."

Tyra's forehead poured beads of sweat as she heard Ghost's name. "I swear I don't have anything to do with my sister and Bullshit setting you up."

"Aww, it's okay, sweetie. Where is Bullshit?" Ghost asked with an evil smile.

"I don't know. I think he has an apartment out in Sunny Grove. That's Co-Co's boyfriend. I swear I don't know."

Ghost nodded at Shadow and turned his attention back to Tyra. Shadow pulled the barbwire cutters from his pocket and bent down over Tyra, putting the tape over her mouth.

"Pleaseee!" Tyra was muffled as the tape hid her plea for mercy.

"We gotta start off with the big piggy first." Shadow, said removing her shoe.

Tyra tried to move her legs and feet, but the zip tie around her ankles made it impossible. Shadow placed the cutters around Tyra's big toe and snipped it inside of a glass jar. The duct tape muffled her screams as the blood rushed from her open wound to the carpet.

"I can't hear ya', ma," Ghost said, getting close to her face as her head shook uncontrollably from the pain.

"I think we gotta clip another one for her to calm down, folk. It just makes them understand that you want silence." Shadow reached for her foot.

"Noooo!" she mumbled with her eyes getting big.

"If I take this tape off your mouth, will you promise to shut the fuck up and tell the truth?"

Tyra nodded and Ghost ripped the tape violently from her lips.

"Now, where is Bullshit?" Ghost asked her through the light cries she tried to hold in.

"I swear. Co-Co's the only person that knows. He only wanted me to set you up and get you to a hotel so he can rob you. I promise, I don't know." Tyra's make up began to smear her face.

"So, why don't I believe you?"

"I wouldn't lie. Please, just look through my phone. It's in my phone." Tyra began to yell, seeing Shadow pick the pliers back up.

Ghost dug in Tyra's front pocket, grabbed her phone and handed it to Shadow. Looking at the phone he began to scroll through it until he read every message from Bull-shit. Shadow looked over at Ghost, trying to give him a slight nod to verify that Tyra wasn't lying as he continued searching.

"I'm going to have to take you up on this one, but in order for you to go free, you still have to choose a brown bag." Ghost held them in different hands.

"What if I choose the wrong one?"

"Then you'll kill yourself."

Tyra looked back and forth between the two bags and chose the one in Ghost's right hand.

"Okay, now let's see what's in the bag you lost out on first." Ghost untied the knot, reached in the bag and pulled the 9 millimeter Beretta out, shaking his head. "This could have been a good defense weapon. "You could set yourself free with an instrument like this," he teased, pulling the full clip out, sliding it back in.

"But I still haven't seen the bag I chose," Tyra said as she started to tremble in fear again.

"Fair enough." He walked over to her with the hidden surprise. Ghost pulled her head forward, forcing it inside the bag as he laced the belt around her throat, letting her hit the carpet.

Tyra screamed as the poisonous snake repeatedly bit her in the eye. She rolled over on her side, breaking her wrist as the snake continued to deliver the viscous bites to her face. After Ghost and Shadow saw her movements stop, he delivered two shots through the bag. He and Ghost then walked out of the door.

Arriving back at Erica's house, Shadow and Ghost got out of the car and headed in the spot. D-Lo, Tim and J.L.

sat on the couch with Tiffany standing against the wall. Suave sat quietly on the right side of the floor.

"It looks like we got a couple of family members to kill." Ghost said, looking at D-Lo.

"I don't get it. How would we have known that he was our brother? Ma ain't ever said anything about dad having another kid."

"Honestly, I don't give a fuck. I remember the man a little, but he was never there to be a father to me. Maybe ma wouldn't have ever treated me the way she did if he would have stayed." Ghost had a non-caring expression.

"Yeah, you might not give a fuck, nigga. But we have enough to worry about in the streets. Let alone our own fucking family is trying to kill us. And must I remind you we don't even know how these motherfuckers really look, or even where they stay?" D-Lo was getting heated at Ghost's mind frame.

"Yeah, but we know how Bullshit looks, and if we find him, we find the so called pussy grandad who's sending all these shots. I killed a man we didn't know was our brother because he killed our mother. Maybe if I would have known, I would've paralyzed him, giving him some mercy. Instead, a man who never showed himself to us as our grandfather appears and wants to kill us. Doesn't sound like family to me."

"Yeah, it may be hard to believe, Ghost, but it's real. The only person who can tell us the truth is dad and he's dead. Don't you understand that?" D-Lo raised up.

"That's a tough pickle."

"You know. just because you don't give a fuck about what's going on doesn't mean I don't. You starting to let these streets control your dumb, ass nigga. You think you get points for killing our own family?"

Ghost put the cigarette out in the ashtray, cutting his eyes at D-Lo as he stood up. The team felt the animosity in their vibes as Ghost met him face to face. "Now what you need to do is stop being a bitch and let's handle business. I ain't had a daddy my whole life, nigga, and ain't finna start now." Ghost balled his fist.

"Hey, chill the fuck out y'all," Shadow said, walking in between them.

"You betta watch ya' self, lil' bruh." D-Lo pointed his finger at him.

"I can't watch shit that I can't see, dumb ass nigga. You niggas can leave whenever you want. But regardless I'm not gonna stop until whoever's looking for me is dead."

"Say, Don," Tim said, catching Ghost before he walked out on the porch. "Everybody just chill and work this out. We fam, and not only that, we brothers."

"I just feel it's something extra to this shit. If this is our grandfather like the cop said, why is he spending so much energy trying to murder Ghost? He's the same person that murdered our father." D-Lo pondered aloud.

"Well, we damn sho ain't gone figure out what's going on if he sending bullets flying at our heads. I say we need to find Bullshit and get his ass to talk. Smoke his stupid ass, then go after this man who's obviously got a vendetta with us," Ghost said.

"So, what you think? We just gonna bump into these people? We don't know our way around California, Ghost."

"We make him come to us. The way I see it, he's been trying to catch us. From officers to hitmen to our own so-called family. If we kill these stupid assholes, who're supposedly looking for us, he will either come himself or keep sending people like a bitch."

"And what if he keeps sending people and never show?" Suave asked.

"Then we gone keep killing everybody that comes in our path until we find out what's going on." Ghost replied.

"Bae, why don't you look him up through the system? It shouldn't be that hard to crack through the data base and find out a little information about him," Erica suggested.

"That's a start," Shadow said, looking over at Ghost.

"It doesn't matter to me. Let's just get rid of these two assholes and see what's up next. I'm going to find him one way or another."

"Send Tay to go and cover the strip club tomorrow. I told Helena to hold the kids until we contact her. I have a bad feeling about this, so let's just go ahead and get this shit over with," D-Lo said, grabbing his gun.

"I got a plan and it's all gonna come together if we just work as a team. This man obviously wants us dead. But if everybody is dead, no one can talk. So, cousins or not, if these niggas can't tell us nothing, it's no point of leaving them alive." Ghost said seriously.

"If it got this far with killing all these family members, they are gonna tell us something." D-Lo was anxious to know what was ahead for them.

CHAPTER 13

Bullshit pulled in slowly to his five-bedroom home. The Pinnacle was an exquisite place to live. The Woods and The Forest around the area are exclusive gated communities in Coto de Caza, Orange County. The suburbs are homes to a lot of married couples, and many homes were custom built with tracts that were still routinely sold. It was guaranteed one of the best communities standing

Bullshit stepped out of his car and headed into the house. Walking into his living room, he made his way through the kitchen where Shooter was playing the PlayStation 3.

"Wassup, bro?" Shooter greeted him, dumping the ashes from his blunt.

"The same shit. I got word on where we can find that nigga Ghost." Bullshit took a seat at the table.

"How did you do that? You must have talked to Co-Co."

"Hell naw, I haven't heard form that bitch in two days. She supposed to tell me where the nigga stay, but now I think she slick working for this nigga." Bullshit took the blunt from his brother's hand.

"So how did you find him?"

"Tyra."

"Oh yeah. I knew her little slime ass was good for a little something. What did she say?"

"She says the nigga doing a transaction with her for ten keys to give to her brother. They supposed to meet at a warehouse tomorrow in Orland."

"Orland? Why the fuck is he meeting her so far away?"

"Of course, you know we been on this nigga's ass, and at the same time Pa is using all his resources to catch him. He's gonna try to be as low key as possible."

"So, are we really about to kill our own cousin?"

"What do you mean? Of course we are. That fucking coward killed half of our generation. He took Antwan from us and he killed Auntie Elaine." Bullshit said with a heated expression.

"But he didn't know."

"Miguel, he killed our little brother. He came to our hometown and murdered Devon on our sister's porch. He needs to be removed from the Ramirez family. Family is all we have, Miguel."

"These are the same cousins our uncle Michael used to bring here for us to be a family. The same ones who have Ramirez blood running through their veins. We are going to keep killing until our family is in the ground, Raphael?"

"Do you want to go against Pa-Pa, Miguel? Huh? You want to get disowned by our own grandfather for a person who's preying on his own family's demise?"

"You mean the same way Pa-Pa disowned you? He never gave us a chance to be family with our own family. So why would he care for disowning us?" Shooter returned, aggravated.

"Miguel? We haven't seen these people since we were like seven. He brought this situation on himself and I refuse to let my family die in vain."

"You know just like I know that this shit is about money, Raphael. What about him murdering our uncle because he felt his money was more important? How can you expect to abandon someone at a young age and think they would know you? The whole time we've been spoiled rich, we had family who were suffering, taken away from the family because of disputes about currency."

"And what do you think we can do to handle this Miguel, huh? Should we let him kill us and destroy our family because of his father's mishaps when he was younger?"

"No, but maybe we can talk to them," Miguel suggested, really trying to be reasonable.

"We're gonna do exactly what our grandfather told us to do," Bullshit shouted angrily in his Spanish accent.

"I don't have to kill my own family for the pleasure of Jesus. You're gonna get us both killed, you idiot. They're just like uncle Michael. They're gonna fucking kill us, Raphael. You know we can't win."

"I wouldn't care how many people they have killed, nor do I care if our uncle was a killer, how everyone says he is. We have to end this now."

"Well, you're gonna be ending it by yourself." Shooter said

The left hand that came down on Miguel's jaw made him fall out of the chair. Before he had a chance to react, Bullshit pulled out his F and N, pointing directly in his face.

"You don't have a choice, Miguel. Pa-Pa paid me a lot of money to take care of this bozo and nobody, including you, is gonna stop me from completing the mission. You either come or you die with him." Bullshit spat, pressing the barrel of his gun to his little brother's nose.

"You're no different than Jesus. Greed controls you and power will make you do anything for the next coin. You're gonna regret doing this."

"That'll be something I have to just deal with." Bullshit released Shooter's shirt and headed for the door. "Make sure you're ready tomorrow." He opened the door, walked out and closed it behind him.

Shooter picked up his phone and did the only thing he could do. The right thing. After he sent his message out he began to think of his next plan. How to leave and never come back to California. Shooter pulled the half-torn photo out of his wallet of him and his brother. Half of his uncle Michael's face sat in the middle with his arm around someone that was unknown from the ripped half of the picture.

"I hope things go alright, father," Shooter said, then said a silent prayer to his father.

Across town, Tiffany and Erica sat in the house waiting for Ghost and the team to arrive from setting their plan in motion.

"Don't you think it's kinda weird that Ghost and D-Lo's granddad has never been in their life but he keeps trying to kill them about something they never knew?" Tiffany asked Erica.

"I think it's weird he has to kill his own family, but it has to be something personal for his grandad to keep trying to have them killed. Think about it. The officer in the basement said that Ghost's daddy stole fifty million dollars from him. He answered to that by having his own son killed. But doesn't it seem weird that the other kids in his family are familiar with their grandad but Ghost and D-Lo have no memories of ever being with him?"

"Yeah, but maybe he abandoned them because of his father's actions. He killed a half-brother he never knew existed and now his grandfather has come out of hiding to finish the sons?" Tiffany guessed.

"No, it's something else. Why would he keep sending his own blood to risk their life, trying to kill Ghost and D-Lo? Why wouldn't he hire any professionals?"

"Ghost and D-Lo have killed everything that has come up to them. It's like he knew that Bullshit and his brother is gonna die. They obviously know what Ghost is capable of. If he really cared for them, he wouldn't rush his family to go and murder more family. It's more to the story than we know. What are you gonna do about your job?" Tiffany asked in a concerned tone.

"I'm not leaving my child and Ghost. I'm not leaving any of you. You all are the only family I have." Erica assured her after thinking about her career.

"So, you're willing to spend the rest of your life on the run with us and give up your whole life?"

"I'm gonna run with the family until I'm in a casket. I love my career and I had a bright future ahead of me, but this is where I belong. This is the only thing I have left to live for." Erica rested her head on the couch.

"Do you feel the same way about me?" Tiffany asked, putting her hand on Erica's thigh.

"Of course, I do, Tiffany. We've been through our differences but at the end of the day, were still family."

"Do you love me too?" she asked, moving her hand closer to her inner leg.

She tensed up as she looked at Tiffany and nodded.

"You don't have to be scared of me," Tiffany whispered seductively while unbuttoning Erica's jeans.

Erica's heart raced as Tiffany dug inside her boxer shorts and touched her clit. She leaned over, sticking her tongue in her mouth as Erica tried to run away from her fingers.

"Fuck that, I'm tired of you playing with me." Tiffany aggressively grabbing Erica's waist, pulling her closer. She grabbed the leg of Erica's jeans and pulled them from her body. Then, she descended Tiffany's body, sucking and kissing her.

"Please, Tiffany, I've never done anything like this," Erica cried, looking into her green eyes.

"Mama gone take care of this pussy."

Tiffany sucked one of Erica's breast as she continued to finger her. Tiffany became wetter from her touch as she used her thumb to massage her clit.

"Ouu, shit," Erica moaned. She looked up to see Tiffany's two fingers sliding in and out of her.

"It's so wet," Tiffany said. She pulled her fingers out of Erica and licked her juices away.

Tiffany raised off of Erica and shredded her clothes. She pulled her bra over her head, showing off her sexy red melons, and removed her matching Victoria's Secret thong, showing her pretty shaven pussy. She then climbed on top of Erica as their mouths connected and sent sparks through her stomach. Tiffany carefully touched her body as she grinded her pussy against her thighs. Erica wrapped her hands around Tiffany's ass as her tongue roamed inside her mouth.

Tiffany turned Erica over on all fours. She opened her cheeks, rolling her tongue down her ass until she reached her pussy.

"Mmmmm," Erica moaned as she rolled her eyes from the pleasure Tiffany was giving her.

Tiffany repeatedly licked her pussy and massaged her lips as she let her tongue roam inside of her.

She slid her thick frame through Erica's petite thighs and arms, placing her ass directly in her face. As Erica felt Tiffany's face pushing inside of her ass, she buried her lips against Tiffany's pussy. They both slowly licked each other as their mouths slurped in ecstasy. Tiffany placed a finger in Erica's ass, making her squeal in delight as she slid her tongue quickly across her clit.

"This pussy so juicy," Tiffany said, spreading Erica's ass wider.

"It feels so good, baby," Erica grunted, fucking Tiffany nice and slow with her two middle fingers.

"Taste that pussy, Erica," Tiffany said, feeling herself coming to satisfaction.

She removed her fingers and placed her tongue against Tiffany's clit. Erica came all over her face.

"Ssshittt," Tiffany moaned, grinding her hips in Erica's face as she pumped her finger inside Erica's ass. She placed her tongue deeply inside of Erica's pussy until she felt her release her sweet cum inside of her mouth. Standing up, Tiffany grabbed Erica's hand, pulling her off the floor. She pulled Erica's head towards her, kissing her lips slowly and seductively. "I want more of you," Tiffany said, looking into her eyes as she walked her inside of the bedroom and closed the door.

Shadow walked into the trap spot's living room with his laptop while Ghost talked to Tim and D-Lo about their situation. "I found him," Shadow said, looking over at the team.

"Who?" D-Lo asked quickly

Shadow looked at the computer as he began to read what was in front of him. "Jesus Ramirez, AKA the God, was born October 31st,1959 to a Rosa Ramirez. Jesus' first arrest was at the age of 17 for a murder over a drug trade gone wrong. According to the newspaper, Jesus was caught with two kilos of cocaine in his front seat after a murder took place two miles down the road. Jesus purchased two of the best drug case lawyers, complimentary of a Ernesto Fonseca Carillo, AKA Don Neto.

"It's says he's probably one of the oldest Cartel King Drug lords, starting in the late 70's. Neto was born in Badiraguato Municipality, Mexico, and held power inside of the Guadalajara Cartel. Jesus was acquitted of all the charges within two months of being arrested. He was back to running cocaine through the US border for Carillo.

"In 1976, after Jesus was released from jail, the crime rate and drug market sky rocketed by forty-eight percent. In 1978, Jesus was booked on drug trafficking, conspiracy and money laundering millions."

Ghost and D-Lo sat back and listened as Shadow continued to spill information.

"He was sentenced to five years for the money laundering and the other charges were eventually dropped. Jesus is suspected to be connected with over forty-six murders around the country of Mexico. His last known address was a spot at the Continuum in South Beach. It says he was investing in properties and vehicles from tapping in on the drug profit."

"So, he was trying to buy property with all of his funds?" D-Lo asked.

"No, he was trying to buy property and sale it for twice the deal to match the amount he was laundering. He was on the road to being one of the richest Spanish drug lords, starting in the heart of Mexico after meeting Don Neto at the age of sixteen. They even say Jesus would purchase rare jewelry and sell it for higher value. After serving his five years, he was released and jumped back into the mix with Carrillo. He continued to purchase numerous of Bayfront condo's and five star pent houses, opening source after source of income. All of that fell apart eventually in 1985." Shadow said, enlarging the paragraph.

"What happened in 1985?" Ghost asked, wanting to know every detail about the man who he was dealing with.

"Well, unfortunately, his boss Corrillo ended up being tied into a Federal Agent being slayed, and he was sentenced to twenty-five years in a super max prison. After Neto was sent away, Jesus fled to an unknown location and resurfaced in the early nineties. He built a new connect with the leader of the Los Zetas— Osiel Cardana, who was born in Matamoros, Mexico. After he established himself once again as the God, he took his three kids from their mothers and supposedly moved them into a secret location, deep in upper California. All of this is read on the file that Erica snatched from a federal base. It's no telling exactly where he is now."

The numerous things that was just read to Ghost made him think harder about who he was dealing with. He wondered where he was and how the fuck was Jesus able to catch every move he made.

"How the hell did we happen to be the ones to have a Spanish drug lord as a grandfather and he happens to be one of the most notorious criminals through the seventies and eighties? It just doesn't seem real." D-Lo said, feeling drained.

"I don't know, but I'm gonna tell you right now, we're gonna need a better plan if we're thinking about going against this man." Shadow said seriously.

"You said he began dealing with the Los Zetas. That was created in Nuevo Laredo, right?" Ghost asked looking at Shadow.

"Exactly," Shadow replied

"So, these are the same people who were dealing with the La Stessa?"

"What the hell is La Stessa?" Suave asked.

"That's what they used to call the new men who joined their organization." Shadow replied, sparking up his Newport.

"You mean the Cosa Nostra?"

"Yes. Truly, the cocaine industry has been traditionally controlled by Colombian's Cartel traffickers. Columbian groups are the largest, wealthiest and more sophisticated organizations when it comes to smuggling cocaine into the US," Shadow said, dumping his ashes on the floor.

"So how the fuck is we suppose to get to this motherfucker if we don't even know how to find him? This is a notorious crime boss who's been sliding away from the system and has been hiding ever since." D-Lo said.

"He can't be too far if he can easily send our own family to murder us. Obviously, he's still in California." Ghost reckoned.

"But, lil' bro, that was in eighty-five when they said he fled to Cali. Do you think he still hiding out up here?"

"But, think about it. The officer told us that our dad was a killer from Atlanta to California. If Bullshit and Shooter still live in California, that's another generation. He can't be that damn far away." Ghost was thinking outside the box.

"He's definitely in California. He's trying to send a direct message and he's not playing around. His money is large and he probably have most of the law enforcement on his side. His connections are phenomenal. We have to move slowly on this. I feel something worst coming than just a couple of cousins." Shadow said, trying to mold the situation.

"We're in too far. He's gonna keep coming. So, I'm gonna end it and find him." Ghost said with murder dancing in his mind. He looked down at his phone that vibrated with a message. When Ghost read the screen, he got up from the table and walked inside the bedroom.

"We have to leave this alone," D-Lo told Shadow.

"I agree, bro. But that's something we have to get through Ghost's head."

"We're about to go against a man who's beyond our league. We literally have to go to war with our own grandfather." D-Lo saw the catastrophe.

Chris Green

CHAPTER 14

Bullshit and Shooter cruised in the all black Ram Truck as they prepared themselves for what was at stake. The country road that lead to the warehouse was bumpy with massive dirt rocks. Bullshit killed his lights before he made the turn in and killed the engine.

"It's only one of him, Miguel. We handle this for our family. After this, it will all go back to normal." Bullshit said, checking his two 9 millimeter clips.

"How do we know if he's even in there?" Shooter asked, looking at the two doors 50 feet from them.

"Because Tyra texted me and said they were making the exchange now. That was two minutes ago. That has to be his car right there next to Tyra's. She said they're alone."

"Fuck it, let's go." Shooter jumped out the passenger seat of the truck.

Bullshit held on to his pistols as he climbed out of the truck. They crept smoothly against the side of the building until they reached the entrance. As they walked in and began to head towards the main room, the lights were disconnected, leaving the area totally pitch black.

"What the fuck?" Bullshit said, taking a step into the darkness from the paranoia he felt come upon him.

"Miguel?" Bullshit whispered, blinded by his eyes trying to readjust to the darkness.

As the room became quiet from Bullshit trying to listen to the movements, he hard thud from the steel bat crashed against the back of his head. The dizziness from the slugger made him crash to the floor and black out.

"I told you we on the way, Mami." J.L. said as he pushed the whip to the 75 miles per hour limit.

"Do you have Ghost with you?" The Spanish chick asked in her broken English.

"Yeah, I got Ghost with me, ma." J.L. grinned sinisterly, looking over at Trouble. "How do you even know Ghost?" J.L. asked, sensing her obsession with his friend

"Who doesn't know Ghost? He owns the Split Decision strip club close to Beverly Hills. Papi is like God to me." The woman said excitedly.

"That's right." J.L. chuckled at her remark. "Well give me about thirty minutes and we should be there," he said, looking at his Hublot classic fusion watch.

"Understood, Papi. We are in room four forty-four."

"Cool. We in motion, Beautiful," J.L. informed her before hanging up.

"Where did you meet these bitches?" Trouble asked, wondering where they were headed.

"I ran into them after I went and picked up some info from his club earlier. I stopped at the nearest gas station to fill up the tank and they happened to pull in behind me."

"I don't know about you, but I'm 'bout to try and record this shit." Trouble laughed.

"Just make sure that shit go viral, nigga." J.L. laughed, giving Trouble some dap as he kept his eyes on the road.

"So, what about the situation with Ghost?"

"Man, listen dog, I just got out of the hospital from being shot up about this shit. I've risked my life for Ghost on numerous occasions and I wouldn't never change that even if I had to. But the shit that's going on now is too deep, my boy. I just took two slugs because of his own family wanting to get rid of him. It's getting too deep. I love my dog, don't get me wrong, and Ghost is a very smart nigga. But it's gotten to the point where he doesn't even want us around any people who are not affiliated, and to stay out of sight from la familia." J.L. shrugged, taking a swig of his Remy Martin.

"Yeah, but maybe he's just trying to keep things tight and secured. He hasn't made it this far for it to be some blow up. He's doing everything for a reason."

"Yeah, but what reason do you have to think you can control everything and not even have control over yourself? The same thing that Ghost tells us not to do, he does the opposite. He actually feels like he is God. When you run things for so long in a certain way, it becomes a habit with your behavior, my nigga."

"True, but Ghost has traded in a lot to be in the position he is in. He's lost family and been in situations where his freedom would be snatched forever. Not to sound like a rider, my nigga, but niggas who been through so much as he has, it's kinda best to have them change."

"Yeah, maybe you're right. But what you gotta understand is everyone still has their own life to live. If I'm running around helping you solve your problems, that leaves me no time for my own serious situations, ya' dig? I told this man I was going to fuck me a bitch tonight, and he said he don't think the team should be moving around when it's so much going on. The man told me it's bad luck to think about pussy when there is a war going on." J.L. uttered.

"And you don't think that makes a little sense?"

"No."

"And you stand behind that?"

"Fucking right. What does your family having an all-out beef with you have to do with me? I'm tired of being caged away from the world because I'm too busy fighting a battle that ain't mine. I'm just ready to live again. I fuck with my dawg Ghost, but it's time to understand that I still have my own life." J.L. said with a serious tone.

"I fell ya', but remember things are made to be certain ways, and when you go against the grain of reality, it starts to get beyond crazy. I would rather flow with the water instead of the water pushing me off and leaves without me."

"That's real, my nigga."

J.L. pulled the whip into the Beverly Hilton hotel off of Wilshire Boulevard and parked his car in front of the entrance. He and Trouble stepped out of the car quickly and handed the keys to the valet. After tipping him $50, they continued to make their way through the big entrance across the floor.

"Damn, a nigga doesn't get to see too much shit like this on a daily basis." Trouble admired the amazing structure of the hotel.

"I know, right? Now you see what I mean when I say you gotta take a little time to get ya' self some fun." J.L. pushed the button on the huge elevator panel.

"I would love to rent out a suite in this motherfucker. I mean literally sit back on some Fat Mac shit." Trouble replied, looking at the beautiful white woman who walked past him.

"Bro, within the next year, I'm trying to buy me a penthouse suite, own me a couple of cribs, and even have a few businesses of my own. I really been planning this for the longest, and the money that I have set up and stashed should be able to last me until I find out exactly how I'm going to execute it."

"Now I'm definitely with you on that shit." Trouble said as he and J.L. stepped inside the elevator. He pressed the number 4 to the fourth floor.

"This one thing I know, my boy. If you really want to succeed and see better, you have to push for yourself until you can't push anymore. My whole life I've always been a boss. But I never pushed to make my own stamp in these streets and world. I was just a loyal nigga with a real heart. I'm finna let my past stay where it is and I'm about to leave this life alone. I set up a meeting next week for me to talk to a consultant about opening up a real estate business." J.L. said proudly.

"I salute that, bro. Real shit. you know exactly how you want to handle it." Trouble was impressed.

When the elevator doors opened on the fourth-floor, J.L. and Trouble stepped off, heading for the room.

"So, have you told Ghost about your plans?"

"Naw, not yet, but in due time. Let's focus on fucking these bitches and having a good night with these hoes." J.L. said as they bent the next corner.

"Now I can handle that for sure." Trouble boasted as they made it to room 444 and knocked lightly.

The latch and lock was undone, then the Spanish girl Sasha appeared from behind the door. "Hi, Papi" Sasha squealed as she walked over to J.L. and kissed his lips.

"Wassup, beautiful?" J.L. greeted her, grabbing her ass firmly. "This is my brother, Ghost." J.L. lied, giving Trouble a wicked smile.

"Hi, daddy," Sasha said, looking at Trouble as if he was edible. "You didn't have to bring your pants at all, Papi." The girl teased, grabbing ahold of Trouble's crouch.

"Damn, ma, no one gave me the memo." Trouble said, instantly getting hard from her touch.

Sasha grabbed both of their hands and led them into the luxurious hotel room. The main room as was laced with a glossy décor of expensive tile. The counters and cabinets in the kitchen were made from black marble. The black double door refrigerator was placed against the opposite wall with a glass top freezer that you could look directly through.

Trouble walked over to the patio window and looked at the amazing view that was in front of him. The scene was something that he wasn't used too. He stared out over the amazing scenery and knew that only real bosses could live this way.

The Latino woman that came from the side bedroom immediately caught his attention as he turned his head towards her. The all white one piece that she wore hugged her magnificent body. Her jet-black hair laid down her back and her ass moved softly with every strut. Walking over to the bar, she poured herself a glass of tequila on the rocks and sat on the couch, crossing her legs.

"This is my friend Sophia, Ghost." Sasha said as J.L. continuously grabbed on her, anticipating on hitting her from the back.

Trouble turned around as he stared Sophia in her blue eyes. Her thick thighs were as smooth as a baby and her breast rested perfectly in the thin material that covered them. "Hola, Mami." Trouble greeted her as he walked over to the couch and took a seat.

Sophia looked at him with a serious face and began to laugh. "Hey, how are you?" she asked with a normal accent.

Trouble was stunned when hearing her voice. She didn't even sound Latino, but he knew that she was Hispanic. "Are you mixed or something?" he asked with a smile, looking at the gorgeous dime in front of him.

"I'm Latina, silly, I was just born in Georgia." Sophia pulled a joint from her breast. Grabbing the lighter off the table, she fired up her blunt and sat back down.

Trouble looked at her with a surprised expression, seeing her inhale the weed. "You smoke?"

Sophia looked over at him, blushing, and blew the chronic smoke towards his face. "Nothing but the best, Papi."

"My name's Ghost," Trouble lied, holding his hand out towards hers.

"I know who you are. I've heard a lot of stories about you." Sophia put the blunt to her lips and inhaled slowly.

"What have you heard?"

"Mmm, let's see. I know what I suppose to know about you. I know that you are a blessing." Sophia grabbed his hands, kissing them delicately.

Trouble looked her in the eyes as she blushed at him. He wondered what the hell could Ghost have done to make these women feel like he was a blessing.

J.L. sat over by the bar with his hands in Sasha's panties.

She took another shot of liquor as she let J.L. have his way. "Are we gonna have fun or not?" She then pulled the 8 ball of cocaine out of her pocket.

J.L. looked over at the uncut raw and tooted his nose. "Damn, ma. You trying to get good and high, ain't you?" He took the powder from her hand, examining it.

"I want us to enjoy ourselves." Sasha pouted, rubbing against his chest.

He looked at her face for a second and back at the powder. He hadn't done it in over a year, and the last time was his first time. It was a bad experience, leaving him in a messy situation.

"Come on, baby, are we having fun or not?" Sasha begged, grabbing J.L. dick through his pants.

J.L. took a deep breath and poured him a shot of Patron. After he tossed it back, he looked at Sasha and nodded.

She smiled, pulling him over to the couch where Trouble and Sophia sat in their own world talking. "Listen bitch, we're getting high, you guys," Sasha said, pouring the cocaine on the table.

Sophia popped it off first. Walking over to the table, she scooped up a small clump of powder with her fingernail and snorted as easily as a professional. She licked her finger, cleaning it all up, then pulled her hair into a ponytail.

"Damn. I didn't know we was trying to pipe up like that." Trouble said, pulling the small bag from his pocket. "Anybody up for some candy?" He asked, holding a bag of ecstasy in his hand.

"Now that's what the fuck I'm talking about." J.L. said as he grabbed two of the pills from the bag and threw them back at the same time. He grabbed the bottle of Patron, turning it up as Sophia, Sasha and Trouble laughed from the harsh facial expression he wore from swallowing the pills. "Y'all playing. Them some real biters."

Within a matter of minutes, they began to open up bottles of liquor as everyone took turns digging their faces in the cocaine on the table. Trouble sat back on the couch as he watched Sophia grind her body to the music that played from the iPad. He knew that she had to be one of the baddest bitches he ever saw in his life. Her ass cheeks jiggled without her barely even moving as she held the joint in between her lips.

"We have a surprise for y'all." Sasha said, wiping her nose because of all the blow she snorted.

"I like surprises. What about you, Ghost?" J.L. grabbed Sasha's ass as he held the bottle of Patron in the other.

"Of course, I love surprises."

"Good, because me and my girl are gonna give you the show of your lives." Sasha pushed them onto the couch.

Sophia still maneuvered across the floor to the Latino music that bumped inside her ear, looking at both the men on the couch. As Sasha came back from the kitchen, she carried a bottle of Hershey's chocolate syrup, a small box of strawberries and a can of whipped cream. When she sat the items down on the table, Sophia wasted no time as she shredded her clothes and stood in front of them all naked.

Sasha continued to place the things on the table and opened them all. Trouble and J.L. looked on in amazement. Sophia's body was extra perfect. Her breast were a perfect C cup and her nipples were light pink. Her thighs were as thick as a stallion and her ass was a perfect bubble.

After Sasha was finished setting up her display, she stood up and began to pull her clothes off. Sophia walked over to the second couch and bent over, hiking her ass in the air. Sasha grabbed the bottle of new champagne and walked over behind Sophia, bending down.

J.L. and Trouble's mouths hung wide open as Sasha began to pour the champagne down the crack of Sophia's ass. She licked up the liquid as she moved her tongue swiftly back and forth across Sophia's sweet spot.

"Right there, Mami," Sophia moaned as Sasha buried her face inside her womanhood.

Sasha placed her finger at the top of Sophia's ass and stuck the tip of her finger in. She then used her other hand and poured some more champagne as she tried to lick every drip that ran down past her face.

Putting the bottle down, Sasha pulled Sophia off the couch and grabbed the whip cream as they walked over to J.L. and Trouble. Sasha bent down in front of J.L. as she undid his belt and released him from his pants. Shaking the bottle of whipped cream, she squeezed the white cap, spreading some across the tip of his dick. J.L. tensed up as Sasha smiled and licked the cream, taking him inside of her mouth.

"Do you know what to do with this?" Sophia asked, standing in front of Trouble with the chocolate syrup in her hand.

"What do you think I should do with it?" He teased. He stood in front of her and removed his shirt.

She led him over to the other couch and laid back, spreading her legs as she handed Trouble the syrup. He smiled as she rubbed her small, pretty pussy and pointed towards it.

Trouble got on his knees as he squirted some over her nipples and clit. After he sucked the chocolate off her breast, he gently kissed her stomach and belly button. Then, he moved down to her kitty. When he placed his tongue over her clit, her body twitched as she grabbed the back of his head and leaned back in pleasure. Trouble swirled her clit around in his mouth as he massaged her light pink nipples firmly.

"Yes, Papi, right there," Sophia said, looking at Trouble slurp up her juices as she became wetter.

He pushed her legs up closer to her shoulders but further apart as he placed his tongue deeply inside of her.

Sasha deep throated J.L. as she massaged his chest. Then, she stood, mounted him and began to slowly grind on his manhood. She leaned in, kissing his lips as he started to pump inside of her. "Be easy with me, Papi," Sasha said as J.L. began to feel her walls tighten.

"Damn, you feel good, baby." J.L. said, grabbing her breast and watching her bounce.

Her hand slid down, resting her fingers against her clit. She began to twirl them in a circular motion as she got her rhythm on point.

Trouble raised his head from Sophia's pussy and stood over her. His tongue had her mind spent. She panted from the massive orgasm he bestowed upon her. His dick stood as hard as a brick as he leaned over, sliding inside her moist kitty.

"Oh, my God, Papi, please." Sophia moaned, holding his stomach to keep his monster from going too deep inside her.

Trouble looked in her blue eyes, removing her hands. He held them against the couch as he kept her legs spread using his thighs. He slowly long stroked her as her pussy gushed from his girth. He watched as her pussy glistened his piece. He moved passionately inside of her until her body relaxed and began to match his rhythm.

"Ghost," Sophia called out as her body quaked with pain and pleasure in one.

Trouble held the back of her neck as he lightly kissed her amazing lips. He eased out of her, feeling himself on the verge of busting, and turned her around. He arched her ass on the couch as he took her from behind.

"Shit, daddy," Sophia whispered, trying to muffle her screams.

Trouble's wood filled her perfectly as he rubbed down her slim waist and back. She felt the tip of his manhood began to tap the bottom of her stomach. He used every inch that he could to fill her sweet hot box. He slowly wrapped his hand around her hair as he began to have his way behind her. Her ass rumbled against his stomach as he dug inside of her roughly.

"Fuck, Papiii!" Sophia screamed as her eyes rolled to the back off her head. She exploded on his rod as he slid inside of her unmercifully. She rested her head on the couch pillow as Trouble continued to have his way.

Sasha continued to ride J.L. until he came inside of her. He was so high off the cocaine that he didn't realized he came inside of her without a rubber on. She rolled off of him and laid back on the couch. He stood up, leaning a little from the bomb sex he just encountered.

"Damn, ma, this coke got me high as a motherfucker." J.L. said, not paying attention to the side door of the hotel room opening.

The bullet that struck him in the neck blew a hole through the front of his throat, making him lock in motion. The second bullet left the gun, shooting J.L. in his head as his body fell lifeless to the floor.

"What the fuck?" Trouble panicked, jumping off Sophia, covering his naked body.

The two men in all black aimed their guns towards his face as Sasha covered her head on the ground. Sophia jumped behind the couch as the bigger man out of the two walked over to Trouble, hitting him in the face with the all black mini machine gun. His two front teeth flew out of his mouth as his body crashed to the floor.

"What the fuck is going on?" Trouble asked with his hands over him, trying to plead with them.

"You know what the fuck is going on, my friend. You should have thought before you crossed Jesus, Ghost." The man put the barrel to Trouble's head.

"Wait, but I'm not—" was all Trouble got out before the gun released, spraying his brains on the couch.

After hearing the last gunshot, Sophia lifted her head from behind the couch. "Fuck, Diego, you could have warned us you were about to just bust in the fucking room." She said to her older brother.

"We didn't have time for that shit, Sophia. We have to finish this and get out of here."

"We're already finished, Diego. Let me get my clothes." Sophia turned to retrieve her things.

The gunshot that sprayed from the silenced pistol made Sophia jump and quickly turn around. The second killer stood over Sasha's lifeless body and pumped two more shots inside of her skull.

"Diego, what the fuck are you doing?" Sophia screamed, running over to Sasha's lifeless body. "What the hell is wrong with you?"

"Sophia, we had to. She's seen too much and Jesus doesn't want any witnesses. Why do you think we got the room in her name? We have to get out of here." Diego pulled his little sister's arm.

Sophia put on her clothes as she looked at Sasha, staring into space. Her heart hurt so bad for her friend, but she was in a predicament that she couldn't handle. "Rest in peace, Chica." Sophia said in her mind while her brother stripped Trouble and J.L. for their goods and wiped the room down.

After they finished, the killers, along with Sophia, walked back through the side door, leaving the massacre behind.

Chris Green

CHAPTER 15

As the lights to the warehouse came back on, Ghost, Shadow, Tim, D-Lo and Suave stood in different corners of the room with their loaded semi-automatics.

Shooter stood nervously in the center of the floor as he finally looked at his two cousins in their eyes. The look that Ghost gave him made his stomach bubble when he looked at his unconscious brother on the floor.

Shadow walked over to Bullshit to tie his feet and place a pair of handcuffs on his wrists. Then, he dragged a chair over to the middle of the room. Afterward, he grabbed Bullshit's underarms and drug him to the chair, to sit him on the seat. Shadow grabbed the rope off his waist and began to tie him down tightly.

Ghost eased his shoulder strap down, letting the AR-15 rest by his side. He looked over at Shooter who stood still in the same spot without moving. "Wassup, Cuzzo?" Ghost greeted him, taking a seat on the edge of the table.

"Chance, I promise I never had anything to do with Jesus trying to hunt you. I know the questions that you want answered. I refuse to die about something I know is wrong. Raphael will never stop because our grandfather has him blinded by the light of money. I'm ready to get away from the Ramirez family. I've been a slave. Killing, taking and many other things for the sake of Jesus' pleasure. I can't stop you from killing my brother today because his mind will not rest until he feels you're taken care of. The only thing I know is, if you do kill him. There will be way worst things that comes from Jesus' way. I remember both of you from our childhood. You may not remember, but we know each other a lot better than you think. No matter what happens today, I'm just ready to walk out the door and leave this shit behind me."

D-Lo looked at him, respecting his words as he felt the truth flying from his mouth. No matter how mad Ghost and him could be, the fact of the matter was that it was all their grandfather's fault. Jesus was the reason they didn't have a father on their side. He's the reason that the unnecessary heat was flying their way, and he was the reason his whole family was dropping like flies. The way that D-Lo felt earlier was replaced with hatred and animosity as he thought about what he wanted to do to Jesus.

"I respect that you chose to call me and clarify this. I understand now that I made an accident of doing something to some of our flesh and blood. But at the end of the day, I'm a very brief man. And for the record, this family crossed me with this whole secret society thing you all have going on." Ghost flicked his cigarette butt and pointed over at Bullshit. "If he's not going to cooperate, his fate is sealed. We've came too far and this situation is personal now."

Miguel shook his head, knowing that his brother was hell on a leash. But his respect for his own brother just wasn't there anymore. His greed was the reason he was in the exact spot he was at that time. Miguel was ready to be free from the torture Bullshit took him through. "Just let me leave. I can't just watch him die in my face. I just want to be away from this."

"It's not just that easy, Miguel. You're not just gonna walk out of here and think we believe that you aren't still going to get away, and there wouldn't be any hatred towards us. You gone have to pick which side of this family you're with. Because if you with the real side over this way, ain't no such thing as walking away." Ghost taunted him as Suave pointed his AK-47 directly at Shooter.

Miguel stared at his cousin in his eyes and held his facial expression. He looked over at Bullshit for a brief minute, then back at D-Lo and Ghost. "I'll be waiting in the car."

Ghost shook his head and ordered for Tim and Suave to wait with him until they ended the drama for good.

Miguel turned around and began to walk towards the exit with Tim and Suave on his heels. After they left from the building, Ghost walked over to Bullshit.

D-Lo and Shadow continued to post up as Ghost stood in front of Bullshit. He smiled as he cracked his knuckles and slapped Bullshit across his face, almost knocking the chair over.

Bullshit shook his head drowsily as his vision set in. When it was clear, he looked at Ghost, D-Lo and Shadow standing in front of him.

"Glad to have you with us," Ghost said as he grabbed a chair and pulled it in front of him.

Bullshit began to grind on his teeth as Ghost sat down and fired up a joint in front of him.

"Where's Jesus?" Ghost asked sternly, blowing the clouds of smoke in Bullshit's face.

"Where the fuck is my brother?"

Ghost hit the White Owl again and pulled out his glocc 40. After sliding one in his chamber he rested the gun on his lap. "Your brother is good. He's not gonna be hurt. For some reason he loves his cousins. He's ready to leave, and they're outside waiting on us. So, we really don't have that long. I'm asking again as your family to tell me where Jesus is."

"I'm not telling you shit, pussy," he shouted with hate in his voice.

Ghost smiled as he jumped out of the chair, striking him in his face with the gun. "See, you're stupid."

Bullshit's face leaked with blood as he tried to catch his breath from the pain. The blood profusely poured from his eye and nose as he blinked rapidly, trying to shake the throbbing.

"We gone try this two more times, and we can go ahead and end this little hardball game."

"I think you're a dead man. Are you mad at the way Pa-Pa did your disloyal, pussy father? You were meant to be deleted from his family, erased until no one could find a trace of you. Of course, I liked my cousin Twan better. He got off the bricks of cocaine I supplied him, and you and your brother just had to come monkey your way back around."

Ghost grabbed the blunt back from his brother and looked at the ground as he took a small puff. "I'ma throw your body in the ocean with twenty bricks of concrete to make sure you'll never be seen again. You're about to die in the next few seconds, and you don't even know it."

"I will never tell you where Pa-Pa is because you want some empathy for your situation. You might as well just kill me, Chance." Bullshit said lightly from the large ache that invaded his head.

Ghost frowned at him as if he was pathetic. He walked over to him, placing the fire of his blunt into his eye.

"Aghh, aghhhhh, godddd!" Bullshit screamed.

Ghost gripped his curly hair tightly as he mashed the blunt into his eyelids. Stepping back over to his seat, Ghost looked as his cousin wept in pain. He looked at the blood that was drying up on his face and now the swollen eye with the red blister that covered his whole eyelid. "I'll tell ya' what. If you let all of this go, come work with me and your brother. Just tell me where Jesus is and we'll all still make millions. It's still not too late to lock this family shit down. I'm offering you a deal of a lifetime. You know just like I know Jesus runs your whole life. Set yourself free. This is the only option." Ghost begged, trying to be reasonable.

"I'm not trading on my family like my pussy little brother. I knew he was weak. I knew he could fall victim. Family's first with me." He sobbed, mugging Ghost.

"We are family."

"Yeah, but not the ones I love."

"Where is Jesus?" Ghost asked standing out of his chair.

"You just don't get it, huh, motherfucker?"

"You just don't either." Ghost put his pistol to Bullshit's face and pulled the trigger six times.

Boc! Boc! Boc! Boc! Boc! Boc!

Bullshit's mouth hung wide open as his blood began to pour from the bullet holes. Ghost walked over to him and searched his pockets. After feeling what he was looking for, he reached inside, pulling out the white touchscreen. Ghost opened the phone and scrolled through the contacts until he found the number that he was looking for.

D-Lo and Shadow followed Ghost as he pressed the call button on the phone and headed out of the warehouse.

When Diego reached his and his sister's expensive townhome, Sophia shoved past him, went up the stairs and slammed the door to her door behind her. He shook his head with guilt as he headed towards his office.

Inside the office, he sat at the table and pulled his phone out to place a call.

"Speak," Jesus said with authority when he answered the phone.

"Jesus, I wanted to let you know the job is done, sir. Your problem has been officially exterminated." Diego informed him, holding the phone up to his ear.

"And is this for sure? Did you witness this yourself?"

"I pulled the trigger myself, sir. There's no ifs ands or buts. To be honest, it was quite easy. Everyone knows that women are bad luck when it is a war at hand."

"Well done. The rest of your money will be delivered to you in a timely manner. My grandson is on the other line. Sit back and hold for a second as I take this call."

"Yes, sir," Diego replied, leaning in his chair while thinking about the $500,000 that was headed to his new bank account.

"Hello?" Jesus answered the other line to see what Bullshit wanted. He knew that it was a mistake to send his incompetent grandsons to handle anything.

"If you felt that you had a problem with us, you should've come yourself." Ghost said through the phone.

Jesus' heart raced after hearing the voice over the line. His skin crawled, feeling the worst as he thought about his two grandsons. "You're gonna lose. You think just because you kill a few people that you will have victory? If you touched a hair on any one of my boys. I will make sure I dip your head in gold and sit it in on my mantel piece." Jesus said harshly.

"You're a stupid old man. You would rather kill your own family instead of embracing us for the blood that we are. You're gonna be the reason I look you in your eyes before I blow your brains out. I'm not gonna stop until I get ya'." Ghost kept the conversation short and brief.

"You're gonna wish my filthy son never birthed you after your last breath leaves your chest!" Jesus screamed putting his cigar out in his ashtray.

"I know."

Jesus crashed his hand on top of the ashtray, breaking it into pieces as he tossed his phone on the desk.

His chest had become hot as he held his heart. He began to cough violently. He opened the little draw to his desk and pulled out a bottle of prescription pills. Opening the top, he threw two pills back and grabbed the shot of Gin to wash it down.

He rubbed his hand through his slick hair and thought about what he would do. Things were beginning to get out of hand and now his two grandsons were probably a casualty to his reckless situation.

He rubbed through his white beard as he grabbed his cigar to light it back up. Picking his phone up, he leaned back in his chair as he placed his call.

"Yes, sir?" Diego answered.

"Mr. Sanchez, it seems to me that you've made a mistake," Jesus said calmly.

"No disrespect, sir, but I don't make mistakes. I carried out the exact orders you asked me to." Diego replied, thinking Jesus must have been playing a game.

"Oh, yes my friend, you've made a mistake because the person I told you to handle still has a soul in his body."

"Jesus, I stood over this man and took his life myself. That's impossible!"

"Yes, I pray it is impossible because I'm really sick of the issue. Unfortunately, he's well alive and you're past dead." Jesus hung up in Diego's face.

As he easily placed his phone back on the table, he knew that it was time to go harder. He refused to let anyone think they were in a higher position than him. Even if that meant killing another piece of his bloodline.

He poured himself another glass of the gin and tossed it back, then looking to his side.

"Romeo, I want you to go and handle this. I want you to bring him back to me and bury him in the backyard. Kill anyone that stands in your way. No mercy, Romeo," Jesus ordered, looking at the man with the bloodshot eyes.

"Yes, Pa-Pa," Romeo replied humbly as he stood stiffly in the corner.

"I want you to make him pay. Kill both of them. Bring their bodies back. Make me proud."

"Yes, Pa-Pa," Romeo repeated as he walked out of the room.

Jesus leaned back in his chair and rested his eyes. His mind was so twisted at the time he felt like he should just kill everyone to make sure his safety was ensured. His main focus was getting his other situation handled and out of the way, but Ghost was starting to become a real slow headache for him.

Ghost was smart and his skills were undeniable, but the man that was heading towards his way was a natural. His skills were the type that would make a man think it was a nightmare until his spirit left its flesh.

CHAPTER 16

The tip of the sun had just begun to rise at 6:45 in the morning. Diego sat on his bed as Jesus' words bounced in his head.

"You're past dead!" he said before hanging up in his face. The threat that Jesus made on his life was past serious. He walked over to his dresser and looked at himself in the mirror. His eyes were red from the Vodka he drank through half the night. He leaned down and sniffed a line of the cocaine through his right nostril.

"You think you can kill the Siniestro, motherfucker?" Diego said as he pulled his Sig Sauer handgun from his waist, aiming it at his own reflection.

He walked back over to his bed to pick up his bullet-proof vest. After he strapped it across his body, he slid his gun down on his waist. He grabbed the phone and dialed Jesus' number, ready to confront him. After receiving the voicemail twice, he crashed the phone against the wall. Lifting up his bed he grabbed the mini Carbon 15. He then made it up in his mind that if Jesus wouldn't give him the other half of his money and apologize for the disrespectful manner he came with, then today would be the day he dies.

Diego walked down the steps as Sophia walked out of her room.

"Diego, where are you going?"

"Just stay back. I'm going to handle my business!" He shouted in a rage.

As he stepped out of his front porch, his brain flew through the back of his head as the 7.62 bullet connected with his eye. After his body fell into the doorway, the sniper dismembered the weapon and left from the roof that sat 200 feet away.

Sitting in the living of room of Erica's house, Ghost sat across the table from his cousin as he flooded him with info about their reckless grandfather's actions. He sat in thought as he listened to every word that spilled out of his mouth. It was one thing to chase your own family down and kill them, but from what the team sat back and listened to, it sounded like killing family was completely normal.

"So how come you and Bullshit just never left to get away from Jesus, instead of being his slaves for your entire lives?" Shadow asked, looking at Shooter pathetically.

"There is more to that than you can understand at this time. Jesus is a very powerful man. You try and tell a man no, who you watched chop up your closest friends in your face."

"What?" Ghost asked, wondering who Miguel was talking about.

Miguel took a deep breath and looked at him. "A while back, we were constant with what we did, but instead of handling our sales ourselves, we brought in a couple of men who we really felt we could trust. The men were some of our close friends since the sand box, so of course we felt it was no reason anything could go wrong. Jesus didn't find out that we had these men working for us until a few months later. He felt that we betrayed him. He was furious, because of our family's reputation and movements were to never let outsiders inside of our mix. It was a priority to him to keep all of our family's business, Omerta."

"The code of silence," Ghost replied, looking in the air as he listened to every word.

"Exactly."

"Maybe so, but how can you expect to have a million-dollar drug empire and not expect to have any workers?

That doesn't make any sense." D-Lo said with his hands on his head.

"Jesus did everything in a certain way. Of course we felt we needed workers to help us move our product. We were receiving over ninety kilos of cocaine every week, and it wasn't a such thing as not selling it as quickly as possible. Jesus was a money fiend and his greed kept the press on us to make sure no penny came up short. It was like he was more worried about taking care of something else besides his own shit. When we would bring him the profits, he would ship every penny off to someone else. If you'd ask me, I felt he was the one being extorted instead of being the connect. Maybe because of the fifty million Uncle Michael took from him." Miguel took a guess.

"How does everyone know if our father did this?" D-Lo questioned.

"Listen, no one has ever put more fear into Jesus' heart than Michael. When I was younger, he didn't try to keep anything away from my uncle. He always had a piece or an input on everything that Jesus had on his plate. It was more like he was scared of your father instead of being a kind-hearted dad. Uncle Michael only came out when it was time for someone to disappear. He rarely ever spoke or spent time with the family. They ended up having disputes about money, and your father ended up killing five of our grand-father's best men. He took the fifty million that was supposed to be on its way to a special plug. That connect was very dear to Jesus. Knowing that our uncle Michael was very intelligent and ruthless, Jesus sent a hit to be placed on your father's head for his disloyalty. It was said that Michael was supposed to come and kill Jesus because of the vicious threats he sent, and Jesus knew his son would make good on his word."

"Fifty million is a lot of money, and it has to be a reason that our dad would take that amount of money just out of the blue for a little dispute." Ghost said, trying to make sense of the conversation.

"Whatever happened, it was something personal only the two of them knew about. The only thing I knew for sure was that after your father did what he did, Jesus began to act more secretive and aggressive." Miguel replied, accepting the blunt from Suave's hand.

"So, this is the reason he didn't want any workers moving for you all, because he felt it was too easy to be crossed out by someone who was so close to you."

Miguel inhaled the Pineapple Kush as he nodded, agreeing with what D-Lo said.

"Okay, but you said he wanted to kill Michael for his disloyalty, but what about when you just said that Jesus felt betrayed because you had men working for you and your brother? You both broke the family code. I guess that must have gotten washed under the table because you're still here breathing." Shadow said, sitting down in his chair.

"The three men who worked for me and my brother were all kidnapped. They were tied with chains and bounded to a rope from the ceiling. Each one of those men were dismembered into thirty pieces and spread out through the middle of the ocean. After killing our close friends, Raphael was beaten to a vegetable and thrown on the side of the road to die. All because he hired three associates to help us make money. Does that sound like swept under the rug to you?" Miguel asked, leaning back in his seat.

"Wait, Raphael is Bullshit, right," Shadow asked, looking confused.

"Yes," Miguel said calmly.

"So, if he beat your brother half to death, why would he still stay around?" D-Lo butted in confused.

"Fear would make people do the craziest things. This was the last memory I had of your father." Miguel reached for his wallet. He opened it and pulled out the torn picture.

Ghost grabbed the picture as the rest of the crew stood around. He looked at the picture of Bullshit and Shooter in front of a white house. The man that sat with his arm around Bullshit instantly caught his view. He couldn't see anything but half of his face, and his eyes made his flesh crawl. "Is this my dad?" Ghost asked with a puzzled look.

D-Lo got up from where he was sitting and walked over to Ghost to look at the picture. After he viewed the man with half of a face, he smiled. "Yeah, that's our pops, bruh" D-Lo said, unable to forget his father from anywhere. "He looks just like you, don't he?"

Ghost stared at the man's face and the resemblance was undeniable. The only thing different was his father's long hair. It kinda reminded him of D-Lo's dreads. "Where's the other half of the picture?" Ghost asked stuck on the photograph.

"I don't know. I found that picture in our grandfather's house almost 20 years ago. It was around the last time I seen uncle Michael alive." Miguel replied, thinking about the day.

"Where does he stay?"

"I honestly don't remember. The last time I was at Jesus' house was when we were kids. I never been ever since. Bullshit was the only one who knows exactly how to get there. All the business, money and conversations only go through him. It's amazing how you can almost kill someone and they will stand behind you as if you've given them the world."

"Were gonna find him one way or the other. He's caused too much chaos to not be handled. Are you with us or not?" Ghost asked Miguel.

Miguel took a deep breath and looked at D-Lo and Ghost. "I've waited for over fifteen years to get away from this family, and to be honest, I'm done putting it past me. I'm ready to go ahead and end this immediately."

"We all need to lay low for a few days. After that, we need to handle this and get the fuck out of California."

"We still have a problem. My older brother and my mother are going to lose it when they find out Raphael is dead." Miguel said with a nervous expression.

"You have an older brother?" D-Lo asked, getting a bad feeling.

"Yes, and his head is not screwed on right. Romeo works for our mother and Jesus, and he doesn't move unless they say so. He doesn't even speak to me or Raphael because they have him so programmed."

"As long as nobody knows, we should be straight, though right?" Shadow asked.

"If he doesn't hear from Bullshit soon, he's gonna send someone. Trust me."

"Don't worry. By the time anyone figures out anything, their head will be in their lap. D-Lo, tell Tay that he's on management tonight for the club. Suave, I need you to go and check on Helena and the kids. Sit with them for a day to make sure everything is safe. After next month, everything is getting sold and liquidated. We're moving out of the country." Ghost said, sitting back thinking.

"I'm gonna take a ride over here to handle what we talked about earlier with the house. I guess I'll take Mario Bell right here with me." Shadow smiled, pointing at Miguel.

Miguel smiled, nodding his head as he got out of his seat and left the house with him.

"Bro, I promise you everything gone be good. We fam. It's only one way out." Suave said, grabbing his gun and heading out of the door.

D-Lo, Tim and Ghost sat at the table in silence while they thought about the mission at hand. Ghost couldn't even remember the last time he had fun or even just sat back with his family. Lately, the only thing that had been on his hands was blood. His mind told him to walk away and leave things alone, but his heart for his father couldn't let him. He never even got to have a relationship with his father because of the messy ordeal.

Jesus made it that way, so it was a choice that Ghost would make him live with forever.

"Bro, I'm not trying to see you get hurt behind this crazy shit. This shit is way beyond something that we could understand." D-Lo stressed to his little brother.

"It's no other choice," Ghost replied as he stood up from the table. He shook his head as he headed towards Erica's room. Opening her door, he watched as she slept peacefully on the bed.

He walked in the room and shut the door behind, to slowly make his way to her bed. He climbed in on the other side of her.

As his body hit the sheets, her eyes jolted open. "Hey," Erica whispered, looking like a Victoria's Secret Model in her panties and bra.

"Hey, baby. What's good? Where is Tiffany?"

"She ran out to get something to eat, and a few other things. She's been gone for like thirty minutes."

"Oh, okay. Are you alright?" Ghost asked, getting more comfortable.

"I was gonna ask you that. Are you sure we're gonna be okay, daddy?"

"Trust me, we gone be alright." Ghost said, laying her head down on his chest.

He wanted to believe everything was okay. But it was just something he couldn't put his hand on. It wrecked his mind just trying to think about. He closed his eyes and slowly began to daydream of the massacre that he would soon create.

CHAPTER 17

Pablo sat in his chair, out at his backyard as the cigar burned in his ashtray. He gazed at the clock ticking on the wall when his cellphone rang. Pablo picked up the phone without saying a word and put it up to his ear.

"The job is done. Diego agreed to our decision," the female voice said through the phone.

A tiny smile crept to the side of his mouth as he took a deep breath. "You never have disappointed me." Pablo replied gratefully into the receiver.

"Thank you, sir. I'll be waiting for further instructions."

"Si, the rest of your earnings are being wired to your account as we speak."

"Gracias." The woman hung up.

Pablo placed the phone on his lap and continued to look out of his patio door. The thought that was on his mind made him feel even sicker. He was ready for his whole life to end. The things that was going on with Ghost wasn't righteous and his heart couldn't let him do the dragging of the deceit any longer. His bones felt weak and his eyes turned more yellow by the day. He prayed for the day that he would perish and burn because of the foul trauma he caused. He just prayed that he could see it before his time was up on earth.

Shadow and Miguel stepped out of the car and headed up the steps of Ghost's home. Sticking the key in the hole, Shadow opened the door and walked in with Miguel on his heels. The smell from Chucc's body on the floor made him instantly cover his mouth.

Shadow moved calmly as he walked over to Chucc and took the circular jug from his pocket. He opened it and began to pour the gasoline over his decomposing body.

"You gonna help or stand there and watch?" Shadow asked, pulling the other two twenty ounce bottles from his back pockets.

Miguel shook his head as he grabbed two of the containers and poured the gas throughout the house. Shadow walked up the stairs and headed to the master bedroom. It was one last thing he had to grab before he torched the house. Reaching into the top-drawer, he pulled out Ghost's white pearl handled glocc and placed it on his waist. He opened the closet door and unzipped the black duffel bag that sat at the corner of the wall. He eyed the money, making sure everything was still in place, and zipped the bag up to sling it across his shoulder.

Miguel walked back down the steps, picked up Shadow's sword from the mantel piece, started to pull the case from the steel, but Shadow grabbed his hand and gave him a serious look.

"Never touch that," Shadow said, removing the sword form his hand and sliding it between the strap of the duffle bag.

"Is it really that serious?"

"Look, ya' goddamn cousin don't even touch my damn blade. Nobody in this circle touches the knife, ever." Shadow pulled the chrome lighter from his pocket.

After lighting the end of the drenched cloth, he tossed it into the middle of the floor over Chucc's body. The flames that started to cover the floor touched the wall and started to light up the path upstairs. Seeing the living room began to erupt in flames, Shadow and Miguel were gone as quick as they came.

Walking into the house, Tiffany closed the door and headed for the kitchen to sit all of the heavy food down. *This nigga need to get rid of these damn workers. I'm not about to be dragging food around for all these sweaty ass, niggas,* she thought.

After heading upstairs, the open door in the hallway caught her attention before she could even take another step. The only view she could see was Ghost's back as he bent Erica over on the bed, slowly penetrating her. Tiffany backed down from the steps and moved to the left side of the wall until she reached the bedroom door. She stood at the opening and watched her man as he sexed Erica. At first, she wanted to get in her feelings for the disrespect but her tired mind told her not to.

Tiffany took a long sigh and began to shed her clothes in the hallway. She slid her shirt over her head, letting it fall to the floor. After releasing her bra and letting it slide off, she unbuttoned her pants and slid out of them. Tiffany eased inside of the room and walked closer to the bed.

The soft lips that Ghost felt across his neck made him slightly jump as he looked back at Tiffany. His heart pounded as he looked her in the eyes, expecting her to blow. Instead, she kissed his lips as she began to rub across Erica's soft ass.

Erica moaned as Ghost continued to eye Tiffany, slowly sliding back inside her. Tiffany placed one hand on her clit and placed the other hand between Erica's legs. She began to rub her pussy and did the same to Erica while sucking on Ghost's neck. His head was going a million miles per hour. Never in his time would he think that Tiffany and Erica would actually be in the same bed together, let alone have a threesome.

Ghost pulled his rod out of Erica and laid Tiffany beside her. Erica instantly locked onto her breasts, sliding her tongue across her nipples. Tiffany looked in Erica's dark brown eyes and shared a personal kiss with her lips. He raised Tiffany's legs as he placed the tip of his member inside her wet slit. As if on que, Erica leaned over Tiffany, placing her sweet cookie on her lips. The whole scene had Ghost's mind blown as he watched his two gorgeous queens show their love and affection to each other.

Ghost looked even bewildered when Erica and Tiffany smiled at him. He knew then it was gonna be a long night.

The club's lights glistened brightly as car after car came through the parking lot. The different foreign cars that sat in the parking spaces looked more like an expensive car auction instead of young, rich people coming to watch the women who had whatever to offer. Tay sat at the desk in Ghost's office as he counted up the earnings from the club. After he added up thirty thousand dollars he sat it to the side of the desk and began to start the next bundle.

Outside in the parking lot the cars just started to settle as the girls began their performances. The all black Charger pulled into the club's entrance and parked in the nearest open space. Stepping out of the car, the man grabbed his briefcase and walked towards the front of the club. The bouncer was so busy making out with the girl in the corner didn't even see the man walk past him into the building.

Getting into the club's main section, the man continued to walk past everyone yelling and throwing money as he headed for the back section. He looked over at Tay standing in the office doorway as he made his way into the restroom.

He walked over to the counter, sitting the cheap brief-case on the sink to open it up.

He pulled out a 50-round banana clip and placed it at the bottom of the SK automatic. He slid on his gloves and tied his hair into a Chinese like bun. After taking the safety off the rifle, he exited the restroom, heading back inside the dance floor's section. As he walked around the corner, the first six men that sat in a VIP section were gunned down.

Bdoccc! Boc! Boc! Boc! Boc! Boc!

The club instantly turned into an uproar when everyone panicked. The music played beyond loudly when Romeo began to gun down the strippers that tried to run off stage. One woman tried to come off the pole after realizing what was going on. Romeo placed a shot to her head, making her fall to the stage and on her neck.

People ran openly as the club looked more and more like a track meet with bodies lying on the floor. Tay walked outside of the office door. He witnessed the entire club in a frolic as the Spanish man gunned down innocent people. If the bright flash wasn't coming from the gun, you wouldn't be able to tell that gun shots were ringing out under the loud music.

Tay ran back into the office, slamming the door behind him. He listened as the screams and gunshots echoed through his head. He dropped to his knees trying to retrieve his gun from the safe. He cursed himself for locking his only weapon inside just because the club had been under investigation.

As Romeo emptied his first clip, he dropped it, letting it collide with the floor. He took the extra clip out of his pocket and inserted it. Cocking the weapon back, bodies were sprawled out on the floor and Romeo looked over at the last witness running out the door. The sounds of screeching tires and people yelling could be heard in the parking lot.

Tay fumbled with the safe's lock, trying to remember the code as the noise ceased. As he finally got the door to the safe open, he grabbed the glocc 357 and turned around. Romeo slapped the gun out of his hand and collided an elbow with his chin. Snot and blood splashed from his nose and lips as he fell against the large safe. Tay tried to blink and remove the stars that were in his eyes. When they cleared, he stared up at Romeo as he held the gun directly to his head.

"Where is my cousin?" Romeo asked with a patient attitude.

"I don't fuckin know," Tay said. He wiped all the blood from his face, trying to regain his thoughts.

"Tu alma nunca fue necesaria," Romero told him with an evil smile.

Tay began to speak, but was muted from the sharp razor that divided his throat. Romeo stood over him as Tay's eyes began to wander to the ceiling. He slid the ace of spades card from his pocket and tossed it on top of Tay's body. He then turned away, walked out of the office and back across the dance floor.

Stepping outside of the empty club, he tossed another ace of spades on the ground before getting into his Charger. He started his engine and pulled out of the parking lot.

Ghost laid in the bed with Tiffany and Erica. His phone vibrated on the dresser. Climbing out of bed, he grabbed his phone looking at the unknown number, and picked up.

"Whoa, who is dis?" Ghost asked humbly.

"Ghost, everyone's dead," Tweety cried harshly into the phone.

"What?"

"The club, Ghost. The girls, everyone in the club is dead. A man just came into the club and started shooting. I saw him come out the men's restroom with a gun. So, I stayed inside the restroom. I started to hear gunshots and people's screaming. Ghost, he killed everyone," Tweety said terrified.

"Where are you?"

"I'm in front of the Chevron gas station across the street from the Super Eight Motel. It's like six blocks down from the club."

"Listen, I want you to go across the street and rent a hotel room. Text me what room you're in and I'll be through there in about an hour."

"Okay," Tweety cried, hanging up.

Ghost slid on his pants and shirt, and grabbed his gun after putting back on his shoes. He left Tiffany and Erica asleep in the bed as he walked out to the living room.

When he entered the quiet area of the house, he pulled out his phone and dialed D-Lo's number.

"Whoa?" D-Lo answered.

"I think we got another problem," Ghost said dryly into the phone to his brother.

"What's good, bruh?"

"Someone just came and killed everyone inside of the strip club. I need y'all to meet me at the Super Eight Motel that sit a few blocks down the road from the club. I'm about to text you the room number.

"Fuck. We all sitting over here at Shadow's duck off. We finna head that way now." D-Lo said, ending the call quickly.

Ghost slid on his brown leather jacket that hung on the coat rack and walked out of the door. He tried to call Tay's cellphone but received an answering machine over and over. After he got in his car, he threw his phone in the passenger seat and pulled off. He looked at his watch that read 1:16AM, and pushed the pedal a little harder, trying to get to his destination. He knew for a fact that if Tweety said everyone was dead and Tay wasn't answering any calls, it had to be a situation on his hands.

The strip club that Ghost had was private-owned and the only ones who knew anything about the club were his two cousins Shooter and Bullshit. One was dead and one had too much hatred for that side of the family to give them any info. He knew for a fact that Jesus did the hit. And if he was the one that did the treacherous act— to kill a whole club of innocent people— then things were officially about to get worst. As Ghost jumped on the express way, he pushed his Porsche Cayenne 957 quickly down the HOV lane.

The only thing Ghost continued to think about as he drove was the whereabouts of Jesus. It was starting to feel like the man didn't exist because of the lack of visual. Ghost never laid his eyes on the man, but the way things were going lately, it was like he had a bull's eye on his back. No matter where they went or how ducked off they tried to stay, someone always found their position and status of their whereabouts. Things were already serious, but the heat that was starting to boil felt like it was sitting right on Ghost's neck.

After hearing his phone go off, he picked it up without looking at the name.

"What room, bruh?" D-Lo asked, waiting for a response.

"Room two-o-two. Tweety is in there waiting. I'm about five minutes away."

"We here," D-Lo said before hanging up.

After Ghost got off the expressway he made a right and headed in the opposite direction of the club. He drove down the street until he reached the motel. He pulled his Porsche inside of the entrance and parked next to Shadow's car. He stepped out of his whip looking both ways and headed towards the hotel door. Ghost knocked one time on the room door before Miguel opened it, letting him inside.

Shadow, D-Lo and Tim sat at a small table, and Tweety sat on the bed with her arms folded.

"Now tell me what happened," Ghost said, walking over to her.

The tears that stained her face were dried up and her eyes were laced with fear. She looked into Ghost's eyes and wiped her runny nose. "A Mexican looking man came in the club and just started shooting everyone. Ghost, he killed Fox and Honey. People were laying everywhere. It was like he was looking for something."

"Did you see Tay anywhere?" Ghost asked with the pace of his heart rising.

"No, when I ran out of the bathroom, everyone was just lying there. I ran out of the front door and found this sitting in front of my car before I got in." Tweety pulled the ace of spades card from her back pocket.

Ghost took the card from Tweety's hand, staring at it. The thick material of it was gold with a black ace of spade on the front. He stared a second more at the cursive R on the back of the card.

Miguel walked over to Ghost, took the card from his hand and turned it over. When his eyes locked on the cursive R, his stomach instantly dropped.

"They know," Shooter said with a terrified look on his face.

The team stood up from the table, approaching him to look at the card too.

"Who knows?" Ghost asked, looking confused.

"Romeo. He's here and he's coming."

"Whoa, hold the fuck up. It ain't nothing but one nigga, right? Why the fuck we just can't go handle his ass and keep it pushing?" Tim asked. He was starting to get mad.

"Romeo isn't sane, bro. What fucking part of that don't you understand? He's been doing this shit his whole life and he's not gonna stop," Miguel returned with a screwed face.

"Can't you just call him and talk to him?" D-Lo asked, trying to find out where Romeo's mind set was.

Miguel laughed crazily as he looked at his cousin. "You guys just don't get it. We're gonna fucking die, you idiot. Romeo is a psycho. He's not normal and it's not safe to be here anymore. We have to go now."

"Hold on, motherfucker, I think you need to calm ya' good Dorito eating ass down and let's think this shit out," Shadow said when seeing Miguel freak out. "He bleeds just like everybody else. Let's just catch his ass and do him the worst way." D-Lo didn't give a fuck anymore.

"If we have any luck at all then a couple of us might survive if we leave. I know my brother, and if we don't take heed a lot of us will be dead in the next few days."

"Listen, none of us are gonna die," Ghost said, looking in Miguel's eyes. "We have to end this shit. After this, we know we would never have to look behind our backs ever again."

"Does anybody know where in the fuck Trouble and J.L. is?" Shadow asked, wondering where they could be.

"J.L. said they was going out to a room or something with some bitches. That was yesterday." D-Lo pulled out his phone.

Ghost rubbed his hands through his hair as he began to get frustrated.

"You know what D-Lo, tell Erica and Tiffany to pack their shit. We gotta send them back to Atlanta until this shit is done. It's the only way we can stay focused. Call Suave and tell him take the kids with him back down to the A. All they have to do is give us a couple of days, lay low and we gone stop and scoop them up when we get the fuck out of the states." Ghost tried to think.

"I'm on it, bruh," D-Lo said, jumping on his line to call Tiffany.

"Miguel, the spot you and Shadow went to earlier today out in Lennox. I need you to head out there and help Woodie shut down. We about to get everybody out of California tonight." Ghost had a plan in the back of his mind. "Whoa, D-Lo, just tell them to pack their shit and you and Tim are coming to pick them up. I'll have everything handled by the time they land in Atlanta."

D-Lo shook his head. Still on the phone, he grabbed his keys for him and Tim to leave out of the hotel room.

Miguel looked over at Ghost seriously. "We have to hurry, Chance. Time isn't something we have right now."

"I know, Miguel. Just go get Woodie and meet us back at Erica's spot as soon as y'all leave from there. We getting the fuck out of here."

"I'm on it." Miguel replied as he jogged out of the hotel room.

Ghost looked at Tweety as she sat spaced out on the bed. "Hey, I need you to focus."

"I'm sorry," Tweety said just above a whisper.

"I need you to take this. I need you to get out of town and call me as soon as you make it to where you're going." Ghost slid a bankroll inside her hand.

"Ghost, please don't leave. I don't know what else to do. I don't have anywhere else to go besides to my house," Tweety panicked.

"Tweety, all I need you to do is get out of California. It's nothing up here for you. Just call when you make it to a destination and I'm going to make sure you're straight. I promise." Ghost said, lifting her head.

"I'll make sure I call when I get to where I'm going," Tweety mumbled as she picked up her cellphone, then left the hotel room.

Ghost shook his head as he began to pull the guns from the black Nike that Shadow brought.

"I hope you have something in mind, folk," Shadow said as he handed Ghost his pearl handled glocc.

He shook his head as he began to help Shadow load the guns. For some reason, he could see the blood of different lives spilling from the task that was at hand. But something continued to tell him to finish it. It was to a point where Ghost was ready to die if he had to. His ties to his family had to be ended. No matter who made it out.

As Miguel pushed his way through the streets, his head ran in so many different places that the only thing he could think about was making it out of Cali and out of sight as he headed over to snatch up Woodie.

CHAPTER 18

Woodie sat in the house counting up the last of the profits. He picked up his phone, seeing three missed calls from Ghost and tried to redial his number. After he didn't get an answer, he sat the phone back on the table and began to place the money inside a black garbage bag. After finishing up he sat the bag on the table and fired up his blunt, leaning back on the couch.

He only had less than an hour to get the money delivered to Ghost so he felt he would chill for the next thirty minutes. Woodie closed his eyes when inhaling the weed, feeling the Kush kick in. when he opened his eyes, Romeo stood directly in front of him with his silenced pistol by his side.

Woodie froze in place as the smoke locked in his windpipe, making him choke. Romeo raised his right foot, kicking him square in the face. Woodie fell to the floor, dropping his blunt. The room was spinning as he scrambled to his feet to make a run for the door. Romeo grabbed the back of his shirt and kicked one of his feet from under him, then slammed him through the glass coffee table.

He held onto Woodie's throat with one hand as he placed the barrel under his chin. "Where is Ghost?" Romeo asked dryly as he looked into Woodie's eyes with a cold glare.

"I don't know, I don't know," Woodie repeated, trying to breathe correctly from Romeo's hand around his throat.

"Why do you people always say the 'I don't know' speech?" Romeo put his pistol on his waist. He then grabbed Woodie by the front of his shirt and began to hit him repeatedly in the face.

The material from Romeo's glove split Woodie open with every strike he delivered to his head. After the fifth blow, Woodie was practically unconscious as Romeo released him to the floor. He removed his gun from his waist and bent down next to Woodie's head. "Tu alma nunca fue necesaria," Romeo said, watching Woodie trying so hard to breathe.

He shook his head at Woodie as he stood back up. He dusted off his black Gucci collar shirt and placed his gun to his head, letting three fast shots rest in his skull

Pwet, pwet, pwet! The pistol whistled loudly before he stepped over Woodie towards the bedrooms.

Miguel reached inside his glove compartment, grabbing his 9 millimeter. He placed it at his waist after parking in front of the spot. He then got out of the car and headed for the steps. When he got to the front porch, he noticed that the front door was slightly cracked. Pushing the door open, Miguel witnessed Woodie sprawled out on the floor, covered in blood. He instantly grabbed his phone, dialing Ghost's number as he ran over to his side. After he saw the gunshot wounds, he knew that Woodie was past dead. When placing his finger on the side of Woodie's neck, checking for a pulse, Ghost answered the phone as Miguel shook his head.

"Y'all good?" Ghost asked through the line.

"Ghost, he's dead," Miguel said, looking at the terrible scene of the house.

"He's what?" Ghost yelled, getting furious.

"He's lying on the floor with three gunshots in his fucking face. He's dead." Miguel began to feel the hairs on his neck stand up.

"Fuck! What is everyone doing to keep getting caught slipping so many times?"

The sound of the hammer of the gun pulling back made Miguel looked up into the soulless eyes of his big brother. Miguel sat with his mouth wide open as he slowly stood up from the floor.

"Hello?" Ghost yelled through the phone.

Miguel's heartbeat began to spin out of control as his brother stared at him awkwardly.

"Who are you talking to?" Romeo asked, cocking his head to the side with a crazy expression.

Ghost heard the voices in the background and calmed down a little. He and Shadow began to listen.

"Romero, what are you doing here?" Miguel asked with his hands raised slightly.

"Where in the fuck did you come from? And where is Raphael?"

"I came to handle something and get the hell out of here." Miguel tried to stand up to his brother.

"Miguel, where is Raphael? Papa said that both of you were supposed to be dead. It seems that you look well and healthy, so where is my brother?"

"He's dead, Romero."

Before Miguel could say another word, a 40-caliber bullet ripped through his knee cap, sending him down to the floor. "Son of a bitchhhh!"

The phone came out of Miguel's hands, hitting the floor and sliding over a foot towards Romeo.

"Fucckkk!" Miguel yelled as he tried to hold the blood that was pouring out of his kneecap.

Romeo ignored his brother's screams as he walked over to the phone. After he picked it up, he looked at the number and placed it over his ear. "Where are you, Ghost? Listen, cousin, your death is not gonna be all slow and torture like. Just come to see me and we can get this over with as quickly as possible." Romeo was trying not to lose his temper.

"You sound like you got a lot of confidence, bitch. You expect to kill a few people and think you can scare somebody? I'm gonna do you the same way I did Raphael. Jesus will be after you. I can't lose." Ghost said strongly.

"You're starting to sound like an over-the-phone killer, little cousin. People like us do things a little more professional." Looking at his younger brother, he placed one shot between Miguel's eyes.

Pwet!

After Miguel crumbled to the floor, Romeo cleared his throat and placed the phone back up to his car. "Okay, Miguel is dead now. That only leaves us. I'm going to kill you and your brother, along with the rest of the slaves you're carrying with you. Let's be men and finish this, please."

"Tomorrow, down in El Segundo. The abandoned construction site. It's only one. You can't miss it." Ghost and Shadow put the guns back in the duffle bag.

"And I'm supposing I will see all of you around nine o'clock?" Romeo asked, looking at his watch.

"I'll be there."

"Good, motherfucker! Don't keep me waiting." Romeo screamed, psyching out before he smashed the phone across the wall.

He looked down at Miguel's lifeless face and began to put on his black skull cap. He removed his thick switch blade from his pocket and slowly cut Miguel's tongue out. Romeo wiped his bloody glove against Miguel's shirt and stood up to leave out of the door.

As D-Lo and Tim arrived at Erica's house, the plan was being set into effect. Discussing the next moves to make, Ghost wanted Tiffany and Erica to leave from California immediately. D-Lo walked into the house, explaining the situation to the girls as they helped them gather all the important things they needed, and placed them in the trunk.

"I don't understand. Why would we go back to Atlanta?" Erica asked, thinking she wouldn't make it through the airport.

"Atlanta is the only spot no one would suspect. We're putting y'all somewhere down in Gwinnett County, so y'all faces aren't gonna be recognizable. Ghost wants you both to lay low, and Suave will fly down to Atlanta with the kids tomorrow. It's no debating with this, sis," D-Lo said, trying to convince the girls.

"Has it really gotten out of hand like that?" Tiffany asked with her arms folded, worried about Ghost.

"Things are past being out of hand. Everyone's life is in jeopardy right now, and if we don't act on this fast, we might not make it to talk about it." D-Lo stressed, grabbing the last bag of money that was to be taken to Shadow's spot.

"But I'm wanted. How am I gonna get on a plane? I have to make it through security." Erica said, placing the Osa Gang skullcap over her hair.

"Ghost already had this prepared." D-Lo pulled the fake ID and passport out of his pocket. "He said when y'all land, stay in the hideout until he gets there. Don't leave out for any reason."

"So, we just supposed to leave him here and hope he's gonna just make it back?" Tiffany angrily asked.

"We gone be here with him. We not leaving bruh side until this shit is done. But we gotta go, now." D-Lo opened the front door.

The girls grabbed their bags and got in the car to head to LAX airport. After D-Lo and Tim dropped Erica and Tiffany off, they pulled off as the girls made their way through the sliding doors.

Tiffany and Erica walked slowly through the lobby as they made their way towards the check-in desk.

"I can't leave yet," Tiffany said, stopping in her tracks.

"What? What are you talking about, Tiffany? You heard what Ghost told us to do." Erica told her, looking around nervously, then back at her.

"I have something that I have to handle. I can't leave without doing this. It might be the only way Ghost makes it home. I need you to trust me." Tiffany said with a sad expression.

"So, you're gonna really make me take this trip by myself, Tiffany? Every time we split up, someone dies. It's not that time right now." Erica pouted on the verge of tears.

"Please, Erica, I have to handle this. Our family is gonna die right here in California. Go get on that plane and I promise I'm going to be home tomorrow night before dinner." Tiffany pleaded, handing over her Louis Vuitton bag

Tiffany hated that Erica had to catch the plane by herself. But if it was something that could really help Ghost, it would kill her if she was the reason it failed. Erica opened her arms, hugging her tightly.

"I promise I'm coming home, and Ghost is coming with me." Tiffany said with a serious face. Then she headed out of the doors.

Erica turned around and headed towards the counter, giving the lady her passport and ID. Her palms began to sweat seeing the two airport police officers walk behind her with the drug dog. She pulled her skullcap down a little more as the clerk for the desk looked at her with a funny eye. After the woman cleared Erica's ticket, she handed it back to her and rolled her eyes.

"Thank you, bitch," Erica grumbled, mugging the white woman. She took one last look behind her before she walked through the security section, to board the plane.

After she found her seat, she stuffed the bags in the upper locker area above the chairs and sat down. She folded her arms and sat back as the tears began to pour from her eyes. Her life was starting to fall into pieces more and more every day. Her mind was so gone she even forgot that she was leaving her son behind. She was furious and tired at the same time. But that one thought she knew strongly ran through the back of her head. She knew Ghost wasn't going to leave her in this world alone. No matter what he had to do, she knew he would get through whatever obstacle he had to so they could have their family back. The plane began to slowly take off as Erica tried to let her mind ease, praying everything would be okay.

Tiffany sat on the bench outside of the airport until she saw Erica's plane take off in the air. She took her phone from her pocket to send a message off and checked her surroundings. She pulled the blonde wig from her purse and slid it over her head, straightening it out. She got up from the bench, and walked across the street to the black 2005 she rented earlier that day. Sticking in the key, she opened the door and got in. She looked at herself in the rear-view mirror before making her way out of the airport.

D-Lo and Tim walked through the doors of Erica's house. Shadow and Ghost sat in all black.

"It's done," D-Lo said as all four of the men stood within the radius of each other.

"It's easy from here. Were gonna kill this bitch and get it over with." Ghost said with anger in his words.

"Where is Miguel?" Tim asked.

"He's gone and so is Woodie. I called the hotel that J.L. and Trouble was supposed to head to. They found them shot up inside a room on the fourth floor. I hung up the phone before the woman could say anything else." Shadow said with his hands in his pocket.

D-Lo rubbed his fingers roughly threw his head when hearing the words.

"Our whole fucking team is dead. Shit has gotten beyond deep. Within this time, I've lost two of my close friends and three niggas whose loyalty was gonna probably be valuable. Jesus is on some personal shit. It's not about Twan or any other control over us. Think hard about it. When people make mistakes, they get handled. He could have been had us killed if he really wanted to. Why would he let us live our whole life and try to blame us for a nigga we didn't know was our family? He's not worried about killing us. He's worried about making a point." Ghost said, looking out of the living room blinds.

"Make a point about what, bruh, because he's damn sho been killing everything that's been around us. He's mad because we're killing off our whole family."

"He's mad because he wants to keep a secret. He's hiding something and he knew with us killing Twan that something was bound to be exposed. He was secretive even when it came to letting his family in certain business. Twan was a man invested with more than Jesus. He had connections all over. And eventually those people were gonna start asking questions. He wanted us all to kill each other." Ghost said, knowing the truth.

"He's right. Obviously Bullshit and Shooter knew more than the average person would when it came down to Jesus." Shadow agreed. "He's so secretive to the point he doesn't even trust his own grandsons. He could have sent anyone to come do the job on us. But instead, he sent his own flesh and blood to kill more blood who he felt would find out something about him soon. He knew that Ghost and you were killers and kinda had it set in his mind that his two grandsons would die from the hands of you two, the same way Twan did. It killed three birds with one stone. Either they would kill you and Ghost, or you both would kill them. Either way, he's getting all the people who knows of his business handled at one time. He's playing chess with all of you.".

"So, basically you saying he's not gonna stop until he kills every last person that's been in contact with us?" Tim asked, trying to really view what he thought.

"That's exactly what I'm saying. He doesn't wanna take the risk of someone knowing about him, his business or his whereabouts. It's the reason he's lasted for so many years."

"So, let's play chess back. He's keeping it in his brain daily that we're stupid. He even took out the workers first just to show us the wrong moves we were making. It's time to get smart on him. I'm ready to go home, so let's do what we have to do and get prepared for tomorrow after this clown is gone. I have one more thing to handle."

As the night slowly passed, Ghost sat in Erica's room as he really thought about Jesus. He really didn't know how he would do it, but he knew he didn't have a choice but to react quickly or it would cost him his life. He wished things could go back to normal, how it was before Twan brought himself into a real zone of no one who gave a fuck and went on about his business. He stepped into a pair of shoes he wasn't ready to fill and came up short.

Ghost inhaled the bud hard as his lungs devoured the smoke. As he exhaled the fumes, he let the animal inside him rise to the surface.

CHAPTER 19
Next night
9:14PM

Ghost, D-Lo, Tim and Shadow rode in the car in silence as they pulled into the rear driveway of the construction site. Tim killed the lights as he pulled inside the small hill and shut off the engine.

Stepping out of the car, they cocked their weapons as they scanned the area quickly. Before they could move, the first bullet came crashing through the glass of the open door, hitting D-Lo in his side.

"Ahh! Shit!" D-Lo yelled, falling inside the car, holding his weapon.

"Nooo!" Ghost said, running towards him.

The next set of bullets began to come rapidly, hitting the windshield and front tire of the car.

"Go! Go!" D-Lo said, pushing Ghost off him.

Ghost, Shadow, and Tim ran quickly inside of the construction area as the bullets carved chunks out of the concrete. The shooting ceased after a bullet curved through the sniper's head, making him flip over the small wall.

They ran swiftly, trying to avoid the bullets on the outside of the warehouse. Entering the area, Romeo wasted no time in squeezing the trigger of the Heckler 8 Ketch 416 automatic. They all ducked and caught the side of a wall of boxes as the rounds from the gun shredded through everything.

Bdoccccccccc! Boc! Boc! Boc! Boc!

"Ghost, I thought you wanted to be a man!" Romeo yelled, leaning behind the wall.

He nodded at the other two henchmen, pointing downward towards the men. They wasted no time coming around the corner and heading down the stairs. More tensions built as the releasing of their guns burped rapidly.

"Shit!" Tim yelled, ducking from the rounds as he fired his Mac 90 back.

Ghost stepped around the box, aiming at a man on the steps and released the AK-17. "This shit ain't sweet, motherfucker!"

Tat! Tat! Tat! Tat! Tat! Tat! Tat! Tat! Tat!

The fire from the man's gun returned, making Ghost jump behind the crate immediately. Shadow looked over the metal wall he was behind and sprayed his gun. The two men consistently aimed their weapons as they let go of all they had.

"You might wanna give up while you got a chance, boy!" Romeo said out loud.

The men dropped their clips and reloaded while taking cover behind the metal stands.

"Fuck you, faggot ass nigga, we ain't giving up shit." Ghost said, thumping his AK-47.

Tat! Tat! Tat! Tat!

Romeo ran across another platform as Ghost released shot after shot trying to hit him. The two killers waited only a second before they were back in action with their weapons.

"A pussy's over here, bitch." Shadow said, dumping his gun the men's way.

He began to run through the pallet section of the warehouse as the men followed, pushing in on his bumper. As Tim tried to follow Shadow, one bullet pierced his shoulder. He spun around and dropped his weapon on the ground. He grabbed his shoulder as he leaned on the heavy crate.

"Aghhhhh!" He howled in pain. His body burned from the bullet. The blood from his shoulder began to pour as Ghost dropped down by, him grabbing his wound.

"Hold on, Don, I got you. I got you," Ghost said, trying to stop the bleeding.

He could still hear the gunshots echo from the men chasing Shadow towards the storage area.

"Ghost, you're wasting my time." Romeo said, moving down another flight of steps a little closer to him.

Ghost picked up his own gun and raised his arm, aiming in the direction of Romeo's voice.

"You gotta look at what your shooting first?"

"You gonna die one way or the other." Ghost said with rage flowing through him.

Tim grabbed his gun, trying to stand to his feet. When his head came over the crate, a bullet flew through his throat, knocking him on the pavement.

"No, No. No," Ghost said, running over to Tim, grabbing him.

He opened his mouth and tried to speak, but the only thing that came out was blood. Tears began to well in Ghost's eyes as he rested Tim's head out in the open, beginning to shoot at whatever he could.

Romeo sat behind the huge generator as the bullets started to penetrate the metal. He stepped out, trying to shoot back but was scraped with a hot one that passed his head and arm. "Arghh." Romeo tried to grieve quietly as he held the side of his bicep.

"Don't seem like you the only one talking 'bout something." Ghost said, pulling his clip out and trying to reload. Before he could get the clip in, Romeo fired two shots, hitting him in his arm and thigh as he stepped from behind the wall.

Ghost dropped down on the ground as the bullets began to make him sweat. He struggled, reaching for it, but grabbed his gun and slid it towards him. As he tried to balance the gun, Romeo kicked Ghost's hand, making his gun slide across the floor.

"Not bad, motherfucker." Romeo said with a giant gash that bled heavily on his head. "You coulda killed me with that shot."

"Fuck you, pussy. It doesn't ever last for long. It'll never be another me." Ghost said, feeling his death approaching.

"Esperas vivir despues de hoy?" Romeo asked, aiming the gun at his head.

"Ni siquiera crees que puedes matarme," Ghost replied with a devilish grin.

"Be sure to tell Uncle Michael hi for me." Romeo aimed his gun at Ghost's head.

The sniper tightened the scope to the max and looked through the hole again, making sure that the shot was correct. One shot could ruin everything if that bullet happened to miss. The sniper's palm sweated heavily as they aimed at the target with precision.

"Ya' know, I've made a living killing scared bitches like you. Go ahead and get one under your belt." Ghost tempted Romeo.

As Romeo's pointer finger began to grip the trigger harder, the pressure from the AX-50 sniper rifle pushed through the top of his heart. His eyes widened as he tried to feel where his chest was missing. The second shot slammed directly in the middle of his forehead, sending him forcefully to the pavement.

Ghost began to breathe extra hard as Romeo's body fell in front of him. He tried to press his back harder to the wall, wondering where the bullets were coming from. As he looked around nervously, his heart loosed when he Shadow walk around the corner, rushing to his side.

"What the fuck happened?" Shadow asked, bending down quickly to apply pressure to Ghost's wounds. He ripped the end of his shirt and wrapped it around his leg quickly, tying a double knot.

"How did you kill 'em?" Ghost asked, looking over at Romeo's open eyes.

"Folk, I didn't do that," Shadow replied. He looked at Romeo and back at Ghost.

Ghost's mind felt like it was playing tricks on him as he steadied his legs while Shadow lifted him up. The pain made his face ball up as he stood on his other leg heavily. Looking over at Tim's body, Ghost shook his head as Shadow helped him out of the building to the car.

Chris Green

CHAPTER 20

After the hitman hit their target, the rifle was quickly dismembered and placed back into its case. Walking through the door of the top deck, the assassin walked down the steps and exited through the downstairs fire escape into the gloomy night.

As Shadow and Ghost made it back to the car, D-Lo sat weakly in the backseat from the excess blood he recently lost. Shadow placed Ghost on the other side of him, strapping them both in the backseat.

"Are you okay, bruh?" Ghost asked his big brother, feeling that everything was his fault.

D-Lo chuckled lightly as he looked at Ghost. "Yeah, lil' bro, but I think I need to hurry up and see a doctor before I die of slow drain." D-Lo said with a small smile.

"Just hold on, bruh. We finna get you straight."

"Where's Tim?" D-Lo asked, looking out of the window.

Ghost's eyes and face said everything as D-Lo looked directly ahead.

"Just rest easy, folk." Shadow said, cranking up the car and pulling off. He grabbed his phone out the vest pouch and began to engage in a quick call as he pulled out of the warehouse.

"He's gone, isn't he?" D-Lo asked, sensing the bad feeling in his heart.

Ghost shook his head and rubbed his hands across his face.

The pain of losing Tim, in D-Lo's heart, weighed heavy. This wasn't a normal street hustler they brought into the circle. It was their brother. The love and loyalty that

Tim had could never be replaced by anyone who claimed that they were actually down for the cause.

"I got somebody going to get Tim's body out of the building. At least we can give our boy a decent funeral." Shadow said as he made a right, heading for the express-way.

"We need to get to the hospital." Ghost said, looking at D-Lo.

"It's already handled, folk. I got someone on the way to Erica's house now." Shadow said, hitting the express-way, bumping the meter up to 95 miles per hour.

It took over twenty minutes just to make it back to the other side of town. Shadow pulled into the driveway and parked next to the silver Chrysler 300. Jumping out of the car, he began to help D-Lo walk in the house as Ghost climbed out the car and followed. The white man that sat on the porch immediately followed them in. They laid D-Lo on the couch and the white man got to work.

Ghost sat at the kitchen table and rolled up the leaf that sat in the jar. He watched as the man worked on D-Lo's wound, moving like the expert that he was. Shadow stepped into the next room, handling the arrangements for Suave and the kids' flight the next day as Ghost sat at the table and blew the weed. His mind was so gone at the time he didn't care about anything anymore. His head led him to believe that he could gain closure for running down Jesus and taking his life the same way he did his father's. So, much that was gained was lost without even trying. They were losing money, more family was dying, and innocent people were stuck in the mix from what Ghost had going on. Being the arrogant person he was made things in his life crumble that he took years to build. The tear that dropped out of his eye was not only for his brothers but also the mistake he made even making the situation worst. He knew the bloodshed that he saw in his vison was real. But he never thought it would be the ones who never deserved it. Ghost let the euphoria of the blunt take him to another place as the doctor walked over, handing him four antibiotics and pain relievers. He threw the pills back, swallowing them quickly as he took a swig of the Hennessy on the counter.

As the doctor began to stich his wounds up he knew that he was done with the entire ordeal. If this situation means that much to Jesus, Ghost was officially letting him have it. His three children ran across his mind along with Tiffany and Erica. He played with his family so much that he hadn't even viewed his kids almost in two weeks. Tomorrow he was going to head to Pablo's and drop off his percentage of his money, and after that he was leaving the fuckery behind him. His energy had come close to burning out and his team and family meant more to him than getting even. The war was over with in his eyes, but deep down he knew that Jesus wouldn't be able to accept his losses.

After the doctor finish doing his duties on Ghost and D-Lo, Shadow paid him a generous lump sum and let him out of the house.

"So how do you feel, folk?" Shadow asked, looking at D-Lo's sluggish eyes.

"I feel like a nigga just hit my ass with a bulldozer," D-Lo laughed, trying to ease the pain.

"It's all good, Boss. By in the morning, you'll feel fully rejuvenated and energized. Just get you some rest, Don." Shadow tapped his shoulder.

"Yeah, but don't get too much rest, nigga." Ghost said, walking over to the other couch and took a seat.

"Trust me, a little rest is what all of us need. You must've forgot you got shot too. I'm ready to get the fuck out of the United Stated and experience life somewhere else."

"We good. After tomorrow, we heading out. It's no looking back at this hole we're in."

All three of them began to wonder in silence at all the tragedy that was happening right before them. It was finally over with. It was time for them to leave this game behind and move on.

The night eventually started to breeze by as Ghost stayed by the window, watching out in case something seemed wrong. His phone vibrated with a message from Erica. He looked down, opening it. After getting confirmation that her and Tiffany landed safely, he released a sigh of relief. The last thing left was to go see Pablo and leave California.

CHAPTER 21

The sun began to rise, indicating the next day. Shadow was up bright and early, strapping on his vest in the living room. Once he put on his shoulder holsters, he grabbed his two weapons and threw on his jacket. His mission was to go and pick up Suave and the kids, making sure they got to the airport with no interferences.

Ghost moved around the house quickly as he gathered everything that would leave with him. He walked into the room, placing the last few bundles of cash in the huge Gucci duffle. He threw the bag across his shoulder as he walked back in the room with Shadow and D-Lo.

"So, I'm meeting y'all back here after this last drop off to Pablo." Ghost said, zipping his hoodie over his vest.

"Let's handle the rest of this shit and be outta here by tonight." D-Lo said from the couch.

"I promise, bro. We outta here by tonight." Ghost walked out of the house, down the porch steps while popping two pain killers, and put the bag in the backseat of the car. After hopping inside Ghost pulled out slowly. When getting in the streets, he cruised off, heading towards Pablo's mansion.

Tiffany hurried and made her way through the lobby of the airport, trying not to be late for her plane. She almost fainted when she saw D-Lo and Suave walk through the doors with the kids. Putting the shades on her face, she pulled her hat down as she grabbed her bag from the search line and headed towards the gate. As she boarded, she made sure to keep an eye from under a light blanket in case Suave tried to blow her cover.

Finding his space and sitting down, Suave boarded the plane with Laylah, Bernard and Mariah. Luckily for Tiffany his seats were in front. After placing the kids in their spots, Suave sat down just as the pilot radioed for takeoff. Taking a deep breath, she let down her hair and eased the hat over her eyes as the plane started up. In her head, all she had to do was make it to the house in Gwinnet before he did. As the plane took off, Tiffany prepared herself for Atlanta.

Ghost cruised low key in his Porsche. He pulled down the street, stopping his car in front of Pablo's mansion. After Sanchez viewed that it was Ghost, he pressed the button, letting him inside the driveway.

Pulling in, he parked his car next to the fountain and stepped out. He grabbed the bag of money out of the backseat as he headed for the door. Walking in, he came down the hallway that led to the living area where Pablo sat quietly in his chair.

"Hola, my friend," Pablo greeted him, surprised from the presence of Ghost.

"How are you, Pablo?" Ghost asked with a warm handshake and took a seat.

"Ups and downs will rain, but not forever. Why the surprise visit and the long face?"

Ghost tried his best to mussel up a fake smile before he started to speak. "Everything's okay, sir. I've been a little busy but I came to bring you your percentage of your money and let you know that I was leaving California for good."

Pablo reached inside his ashtray and grabbed his gold lighter. Then he puffed his cigar until it came to life.

"Is there any specific reason you are departing from our business?" Pablo asked, worried if Ghost knew who he was.

"Oh no, Pablo. Business has been perfect as always. A lot of things have happened in the mix of me being here. I feel like that more pain will break my family apart. I just don't have time for that right now."

Pablo looked at him with hurt in his eyes. He wished that he could say the things he truly needed to instead of keeping him in the blind. The connection he and Ghost had was deeper than a plug for drugs, and it was a little too difficult to explain so he decided to leave it alone. "Is there anything you need help with?" Pablo asked with a sincere expression across his face.

"You've done enough, Pablo."

"I have something for you." Pablo put out his cigar in the ashtray.

Ghost sat back down on the couch as he pulled something off the desk in front of him. Standing up, he walked over to Ghost and placed a piece of paper in his hand. Ghost looked at the set of numbers confusingly and back up at Pablo.

He smiled as he looked down at Ghost. "Those are the numbers to you a private account in the Virgin Islands. Its three million dollars waiting for you whenever you get there."

As Ghost stood off the couch, he grabbed Pablo into a hug and thanked him. He respected him as more than a businessman. He respected him on a father's level. The game was all about blessing the upcoming with the knowledge so they can know who to break bread with when they finally got their chance to make it where they were going. It was meant to be passed down to the ones who could really handle it.

"I promise, Pablo, I will stay in contact the whole way. No matter what I decide to do or go." Ghost said with a bright smile.

"I have one more thing for you," Pablo said, putting another piece of paper in Ghost's other hand, balling it up. "If you ever run into trouble or need help, or if something ever happened to me and you couldn't get in contact, go to this man and tell him Pablo sent you."

Ghost opened up the paper looking at the name and the address written in cursive. His heart stiffened and locked as he looked back up at Pablo.

"Sometimes things are unable to avoid. You have to confront them head on in order to move past that situation. We all make a choice in life and that choice is one you have to live with forever because it can never be changed. Please be careful, Ghost." Pablo said, lighting up his cigar again.

Ghost looked down at Jesus' address again and nodded his head at Pablo, then walked out of the door.

Getting back in his car, Ghost came out of Pablo's lot like a mad man.

He pushed the Cayenne 957 forcefully as the thought of murder ran through his brain. He knew that he should just go to the house and meet Shadow and D-Lo so they could leave. He knew that if he told them he had just gotten Jesus' address they would still say to leave it alone. So much was already torn that it truly didn't make a difference anymore with Ghost. He was tired of risking family in the mix of something that he knew was personal. If Jesus wanted Ghost's head so bad, he was coming headfirst.

As D-Lo and Shadow made it back to the house, they parked on the side of the road and hopped out.

"Did you see the same thing at the airport that I saw or am I trippin'?" Shadow asked with a raised eyebrow.

"You mean Tiffany trying to hide at the main counter?" D-Lo returned on point.

"Exactly. I thought we put them on a plane last night?" Shadow cleared his throat.

"That's the part that I'm trying to get straight inside my head. it's something funny going on."

"Beyond funny. Ghost was supposed to been back here by now. The flight leaves at twelve o'clock tomorrow. We have to gather the rest of the money from my house and have it expressed today so it can make it back to the city when we arrive. The rest of the money is gonna have to be carried through the airport." Shadow said.

"If that's the only way, fuck it. I'm just ready to get the fuck out of here. I'm lucky that bullet grazed me and went straight through. I could be fucking dead. I couldn't help but to think about Tim last night."

"I know, folk," Shadow nodded.

"I made sure that his body gets to Atlanta so we can at least give him a decent burial. None of this was meant to happen, bro. But you can't stop something that was unstoppable. We just gotta get Ghost and get the fuck out of here." Shadow dialed his number. Ghost's phone went straight to voicemail twice as Shadow began to think. "I hope he didn't go off exploring. Let's just go and come back. He should be here." Shadow said as him and D-Lo got back in the car.

Ghost sat in the hotel room as he loaded up his black MP5 machine gun. He grabbed the silencer, screwing it on, and began to load his white glocc. He flashed back at the heartache that Jesus brought upon his family. He thought about Tim, he thought about J.L., and he even thought about the Black Team crew's losses while in California. He wanted to make it all worth it. Ghost sat back in the chair as he meditated, trying to clear his mind.

CHAPTER 22
10:00PM McArthur Shasta, California.

Ghost felt his phone vibrate for the 10th time and powered it down. He jogged as fast as he could through the small wooded path, ending up on the side of the massive house. The two bodyguards who sat in front puffed on brown cigars as they spoke back and forth in Spanish.

Ghost crept swiftly, placing his frame on the side of the house and around the edge of the perimeter, looking around the long corner. He could hear their voices clearly as he aimed his gun directly at them.

Jesus sat in the open room office at his desk after closing the top of his computer. He reached for a small glass bowl with a sliver lid. Removing the top, Jesus put his fingernail inside and snorted the pure Columbian cocaine through his nostrils. Leaning his head back from the rush, he wiped his nose and took his shot of his whisky. Picking up his pack of smokes, he fired up one and grabbed the newspaper in front of him. He opened it, looking at the soccer section for a second and flipped to the stocks status.

Dumping ashes to his cigarette, he cut his eyes seeing the top of the gun in his view. Jesus slowly pulled the news read from his face as he stared into the eyes of his grandson.

Ghost's eyes were locked in on Jesus' pupils and he could smell the fear coming off his bones.

Inhaling another whiff of his cigarette Jesus, sat back and stared at Ghost. "Now that you're here, I suppose you want me to beg for my life?" Jesus asked with his thick accent.

"No, I just wanna see you lose your life." Ghost said, cocking the hammer to the gun back quickly.

"You've spent your whole time trying to fight against me instead of working with me. You're the reason our entire enterprise will be exposed and go down the drain. You're nothing, just like your father." Jesus spat, taking off his glasses.

"Must have been passed through generations. See it's a big difference. I got nothing to lose. You took my dad, you took pieces of my life away, and expected for me to crash and burn. You're mad because we survived it. You hate to see anyone who can do it without you, and that's where you fucked up when you climbed this tree."

"I did what I felt I had to so I can keep my business going. Regardless of the way you feel, this movement is the way I eat. And business doesn't stop in my book when you are a true businessman."

Ghost removed his second pistol as a Spanish woman walked around the corner with a cup of tea in her hand.

"Pa-Pa, I made you some more tea." After raising her head, seeing Ghost standing directly in front of Jesus, Eva let the cup crash to the floor, covering her mouth.

"Who the fuck are you?" Ghost asked with a hushed tone as he pointed his other weapon in her direction.

"Please, Chance, this has been going on long enough," the woman said, holding her hands in the air.

"I said who the fuck are you?"

"I'm your auntie Eva, your father is my brother. I'm begging you please, put the gun down. You've killed half of your own bloodline for something that amounts to nothing."

"Eva, that's enough. He needs to know nothing of business dealing with this family," Jesus shouted with anger.

"Pa-Pa, just end it. Look at what's happening!" Eva yelled, seeing her nephew maturely as a grown man, bearing down on her father, ready to take his life.

Jesus looked over at Ghost as a bead of sweat dripped down his forehead. "You have a choice to make son. You can kill me now and have no response at all, but it won't stop, Chance. You can come home where you belong. You and Deangelo, you were meant to be raised the right way, son. Not wild and reckless. Come run a business you were built for before you crumble your own world on top of your head," Jesus said, trying to reason with Ghost.

"Nothing will change my actions I came to complete. I've lost blood, patience, and friends because of you neglecting us. You wanted me and now I'm here."

"Please, Chance, enough people have suffered already. We all can just end this now. Pa-Pa, just end it. Tell him the truth!" Eva cried.

Jesus' blood began to boil as he grew overheated. "You think you will live after you've done this but you are sadly mistaken. You want to know what I did to your piece of shit father?"

Ghost's hand gripped his pistol tighter when hearing Jesus mention him.

"You want me to tell you how I made him suffer?" Jesus smiled.

The rage that build inside of Ghost released as he fired two shots into Jesus' skull.

Boc! Boc!

"Pa-Paaa!" Eva screamed, running to his body as it curled over in the chair.

Ghost watched as Eve held Jesus' head, crying as she mumbled in Spanish. Before she was able to say anything to him, he was gone, making his way through the backyard.

A million thoughts ran through Eva's head as she poured tears from her eyes. She didn't know what else to do. It was impossible to keep a lie going any longer. She rushed to her feet as she made her way to the door that led to the basement. Opening it up, Eva quickly walked downstairs, making her way to the old model TV that sat in the corner. Turning the power knob to the television, the cornered wall in the room began to slide back. The dust from the wall polluted the room as it revealed the humongous silver chamber. Eva wiped her tears as she walked to the door, turning the gigantic medal latch.

Michael sat on the bed as he stared at the four walls of the room. The thoughts of his children and family ran through his head every second as it did for the past twenty years. He looked at the half of picture in his hand and dropped his head. He didn't know where he was, or even who had him. The only thing he could remember was the day he was heading back home to his kids, he was knocked unconscious. The next time he woke up he was in this room and had been for almost two decades.

The only thing he mapped out every day was his food came in bundles to last for weeks. It was slid down through the vent that sat on the high ceiling above him. He never heard any voices or physically saw anyone. Just the thought of it began to make him have a black out episode. He sat in the corner as he began to clench his jaws.

The loud noise made Michael jump to his feet as his eyes bulged in panic. He thought he may have been hearing noises or hallucinating until he heard the latch to the door unlock. His heart beat tremendously fast as he began to black out.

As Eve slid the latch all the way back, she twisted the handle, opening the medal chamber's door. "Michael," she whispered, trying not to step too close in the dim room.

The hand that came out and grabbed her throat made her gasp as she looked at her younger brother's hand. The dead look in his eyes told Eva he wasn't in his right mind. His tightened his grip as he stepped out of the room, pulling her closer to him.

"Michealll!" Eva said through chocking. She hit his arm repeatedly as she tried to wake him from the hypnotized state he was in. "It's Eva Michael," she said, starting to feel herself fade in and out.

Eva built as much strength as she could and slapped Michael's face, scratching him across his cheek. He rapidly blinked as he released her to the ground, after shaking his head. He tried to catch his breath as he looked around. He looked behind him at the open cage and back at his sister on the ground. His heart skipped a beat seeing her face. The last time he saw her, she was twenty-one and just starting to grow over four feet.

"Eva?" Michael asked, bending down to look in her eyes with pain in his.

She began to slowly gain her composure as she nodded. Michael grabbed her, tightly embracing her in a hug as he kissed her head. He moved her hair out of her face, staring at her.

"Where are we?" Michael asked, wondering where his sister appeared from.

"We're at home, Michael."

"But, I've been gone. I left you all. How did I get here?" Michael asked, confused.

"Pa-Pa put you here, Michael. He had you kidnapped after you killed his men and took his money. He wanted to kill you but he didn't. He put you in a steel chambered room and left you there."

Michael's look went from confused to psychotic. "How long have I been in there?"

"You've been in there almost twenty years, Michael," Eva said, holding her head down.

Hearing twenty years made Michael's heart shatter as he held his forehead. The thought of Chance, Deangelo and Twan ran through his mind as he realized how long he'd been away from them. It all began to comeback slowly as Michael remembered the stash that he had buried. The thought of his older brother being murdered popped back into his brain.

"Where is Pa-pa, Eva?" Michael asked with a stern face.

"He's dead, Michael."

"What?" Michael said. lifting her head. "Eva, what happened to Pa-Pa?"

"Your son came and killed him twenty minutes ago in the living room upstairs," Eva confessed with fire dancing in her eyes.

"Is this some kind of joke?" Michael asked her, thinking he heard her incorrectly.

"Your son Chance just came and murdered your father upstairs in our living room. I didn't know what else to do Michael. Pa-Pa told me he would kill me if you ever disappeared from that cell. Your sons Chance and Deangelo has wiped out the entire side of our family, including your own son Antwan."

Michael was becoming dizzy as Eva filled him in on all the information. It was no way that his two boys were doing this. He knew his disappearance played a part in it, but his heart couldn't lead him to believe his two other children went against their own family. "Where are they?"

"Pa-Pa said that they were in a house in west Los Angeles on Butler Avenue.

Michael walked away from his sister and began to climb the steps. After Eva trailed him, giving him everything he needed, he told her to pack her things and make her way to leave Cali. Tucking the pistol off in his waist, he walked to the door and stopped hearing his sister's voice.

"Your son's name isn't Chance, it's Ghost. Michael, something is wrong with that boy, please be careful," Eva said, happy to see her little brother back into the world. Michael slid on his hoodie and walked out of the door.

Chris Green

CHAPTER 23

Ghost drove at a medium pace when getting off the expressway and making a right turn. He pulled out his cellphone and turned the power back on, watching the missed calls across the screen. He just smiled and texted Erica and Tiffany, letting them know he would be home bright and early in the morning. Pulling down Erica's street, Ghost grabbed his half of blunt, sparking it as he parked next to Shadow's car.

He stepped out of the car, taking a deep breath as he shut the door behind him. Walking up the porch steps, he unlocked the door to the house and walked in. Shadow sat at the table, looking at Ghost in silence as he came in, sitting down on the couch.

"Bruh, where the fuck was you?" D-Lo was holding his phone as he entered the house.

Ghost continued to smoke the joint as he soaked all the lessons he learned inside his brain. He looked over at Shooter and D-Lo, giving them a small head nod and continued to smoke his joint.

"Did you at least finish what you had to do?" Shadow asked, knowing it was no talking to Ghost.

"It's over," Ghost said with a satisfied smile.

D-Lo's chest relieved quickly as the words left his brother's mouth. He knew that his brother was a mastermind when it came for plans to go correctly. He didn't know what Ghost did, but he knew if he said it was officially over, then it was done.

"Let's just lay back and catch this flight tomorrow," Ghost said, removing his black force strap vest.

Things came together as quickly as it fell. Ghost was so ready to get home to his kids and a normal lifestyle. In a certain way, Ghost felt that he made the best move and still came out on top, even though there were some losses in the mix.

Ghost, Shadow, and D-Lo sat in the house the next morning as the rain and thunder erupted through the grey sky.

"Folk, you know I'ma tap in as soon as I come from Michigan. I gotta make a quick stop for Megan and I'm back in your rearview," Shadow said, giving Ghost and D-Lo a brotherly hug.

"You know we leaving Atlanta as soon as I get back down there. I was thinking the Virgin Islands." Ghost smiled.

"If that's where the road leads us, folk, then I'ma have to ride that wave." Shadow tightened up his coat and walked out into the rain.

D-Lo and Ghost sat back in the house after Shadow left and fired up a blunt. They had two hours before their private plane reached the airport, thanks to Pablo. Their new house in the Virgin Islands was already being reconstructed in at that second. Ghost took it upon himself to set the path that he made for his family. If it was meant for them then it will be on a level of business and money. He decided to keep his hands clean and pay the small league to handle the dirty work. He was going kick back and live like the don that he is and stay out of view.

"You ready to get the fuck outta here?" Ghost asked, grabbing his duffle bag off of the floor.

"Yeah, bruh. I'ma grab my other two bags and meet ya' at the car," D-Lo said as he headed upstairs

Ghost shook his head as he grabbed his gun and walked outside towards the car. Moving to the trunk, he dropped the heavy bag as he took the key out of his pocket to open it.

The rain dripped a little hard but Ghost knew he wasn't just seeing things. A man dressed in black was approaching him with a pistol in his hand. Ghost wasted no time pulling his Sig Sauer from his waist band, pulling his trigger.

Boc! Boc! Boc! Boc! Boc!

The man quickly slid behind the parked Tahoe truck as Ghost released shots toward his way. He leaned from behind the truck, firing three shots that breezed past Ghost's head.

"Shitt!" Ghost yelled, hitting the ground. He aimed his gun and pulled round after round from his clip, letting off into the side of the truck.

Boc! Boc! Boc! Boc! Boc! Boc!

D-Lo came outside, gun in hand, as he began to shoot at the man who he slick spotted across the street. Then he ran over to Ghost and helped him up off the ground.

"I just want to talk!" the man yelled raising his gun in the air from behind the truck.

Ghost and D-Lo continued to aim their pistol as the man walked from behind the car and placed his pistol on the ground. He raised his hands in the air as he slowly stepped in the middle of the street. Ghost and D-Lo wasted no time pushing forward as the man stood in the open with his hands up.

As Ghost and D-Lo got closer, they could see that the man's hoodie covered his face and he was drenched from the heavy rain. Ghost kept his finger on the trigger as he stood fifteen feet away from the man.

Pulling his hoodie off, Ghost's chest caved in to his feet. He knew that the moment that was happening at that second was unreal. His wrist began to shake as he loosened his fingers, dropping his gun.

D-Lo pushed right behind Ghost's heels and locked eyes with the man in front of him. "There's no way in fuck," D-Lo said with a scared expression on his face as he walked closer to the man. "Dad?" D-Lo asked on the verge of tears.

Michael nodded as he looked at him. "It's me son. I know it seems unreal, but it's me."

The tears instantly began to come from D-Lo's eyes as he walked over and grabbed his father, hugging him tightly. "It's impossible. We thought you were dead, pop." D-Lo said, not trying to let his father go.

Ghost walked over to his father and looked him in the eyes. It was almost as if he was staring in a mirror. Michael raised his arm to Ghost as he looked at him,

"Where were you?" Ghost asked, breaking down with a face full of tears. "You're supposed to be dead. How could you be here in this spot right now?"

"I don't know yet, son. It's really not easy to explain. Just give me a chance to tell you what's going on."

D-Lo nodded as Ghost continued to eye his father, thinking he was about to wake out of his dream.

CHAPTER 24

"I don't get it. So you want me to believe Jesus had you locked in a basement for twenty years?" Ghost asked, wanting to trust what he was saying.

"Yes, son. My dad was an evil person when it came to money, but I was also a hell boy when it came to taking care of you all. My father denied me access money because I went and got two black females pregnant which is you guys' mother, and Twan's mother. He denied me things I needed to survive, so I felt that he was crossing me out. I killed five of his men and ran off with fifty million dollars. I was headed back home to get you guys so we could leave, but I was knocked out and kidnapped. When I woke up, I was in the room and never saw a face until your auntie just opened the door twenty years later. This is the last memory I had of everything," Michael said, pulling out the picture of D-Lo, Ghost, and Twan in front of a white house.

Ghost's mouth hung wide open as he looked at the half of a picture in front of him. He pulled his wallet out of his pocket, pulled out the other half that Miguel gave him, and placed it together. The full picture was D-Lo, Miguel, Raphael, plus Ghost and Twan standing side by side with their arms around each other. Their father was in the middle of their picture with a smile as he held them all around.

"You believe me now?" Michael asked, looking over at Ghost.

Ghost stared down at the picture and knew for a fact that his father wasn't lying. The sight of Twan and Bullshit's face in the picture made his flesh crawl. It was beyond being close. They were literally forced away from each other as children, which is why things occurred the way they did.

"So, I'm guessing you already know what's going on?" Ghost asked, trying to see how his dad felt.

"Yeah, son, I know, but I can't fault you for something that was never meant for you and Deangelo."

"So, what do we do now?" D-Lo asked with an excited grin.

"We have a flight to catch in the next thirty minutes. We're picking up the rest of our family in Atlanta and we're leaving the states for good. You can just come with us, pop. I have enough cash to last us forever," Ghost said, trying to see where his dad's mind frame was.

"I haven't seen you guys since you were children. I've been missing for a lot of different things, but I'm not missing anymore. Plus, I got to go to Atlanta anyway." Michael pulled on his Newport.

"Why? What you have to do in the city?" D-Lo asked, thinking he sounded like Ghost with excuses.

"My fifty million dollars," Michael replied, taking the last of his Grey Goose down.

"Well, let's get the fuck outta here and go catch this plane," Ghost said. He finished getting their things together and locked down Erica's house.

Driving towards the airport, Ghost looked at his dad through the rearview mirror as he observed everything about him. They got to the airport in due time as the Spanish man out front led them through the side door. As they walked through the hanger, the man walked over to the G5 400. After loading up, they buckled their seatbelts as the pilot wasted no time by getting in the air. After having a few rounds of champagne, Ghost began to feel like everything just might be okay, if they kept it this way. Before they knew it, the plane landed in Atlanta after all the talking and sleeping they did. It took a second, but when they got their stuff together, they headed outside to the tinted Dodge Challenger and hopped in to head towards the Gwinnet city limits.

Chris Green

CHAPTER 25
Brooklyn New York
Flat Bush & 96 & Clarkston

O.G. Lockz sat in his apartment in the crown heights as he listened to the loud police sirens. His woman tried to drain everything while his boss was telling him the business of their new situation at hand.

Cat slobbered on Lockz's dick as she held a blunt in the other hand. She deep throated him as she sucked harder.

"Mmm." Cat moaned as Lockz nutted in her mouth, letting her go about her business.

Lockz got on his phone, calling Pooch as he listened to the ringing.

"What it do, son?" Pooch answered, counting the dough he had in his hands.

"Listen, I need you and Dev to take a trip for me somewhere. This job gone be paying triple times what we usually catch for. I need y'all to make this trip to Atlanta to take care of something and come back, B. You think you can glide with that yo'?" Lockz asked, seeing if he and Pooch were ready to move.

After getting his confirmation that they were ready, he began to put the second part of his plan into effect. After puffing on his white widow, he dialed a number into his cellphone and pressed the call button, putting it towards his ear.

The black Challenger came to a halt in front of the four-bedroom home as D-Lo backed in carefully. Getting out of the car, Ghost walked in the house, seeing Tiffany with the kids in the living room.

"Hi, baby!" Tiffany gave Ghost a fat, wet kiss. "I missed the fuck out of you."

"Hi, daddy," Mariah said, grabbing on to Ghost's leg.

"Hey, daddy baby. What has my little pumpkin been doing?" Ghost asked, making Mariah giggle.

Tiffany laughed as Ghost walked over to Laylah and Bernard, getting in their face for a second. D-Lo and their father came through the house as Ghost got himself settled with the kids. After he finally left them alone, he walked over to his dad and introduced him to Tiffany and Suave.

"Where the fuck is Erica?" Ghost asked, looking annoyed.

"She went out to the grocery store about a few hours ago. She might be on her way back by now," Tiffany said, knowing Ghost was about to blow.

"I thought I said specifically not to go anywhere. Y'all act like little simple ass instructions is so hard." Ghost snapped instantly, catching an attitude. He shook his head at the nonsense. He didn't understand. Sometimes the best plans will go to waste all because of somebody who didn't pay attention. Ghost felt his phone vibrate and looked at the unknown number.

"Whoa," he answered, trying to blow the little messy move off.

"Yo, my nigga, I'm calling about that paper," Lockz said as he held the phone, waiting for a reply.

"Who the fuck is this?"

"This Lockz, B. I'm calling about the paper your granddad owes my boss, son."

"Fuck my granddad and whatever he owed you. I ain't got shit to do with whatever y'all had going on." Ghost said, feeling insulted.

"Well, my nigga, unfortunately your granddad owes my boss two hundred kilos of cocaine. It's been three weeks since the shipment was placed and handled, and the drugs still haven't been delivered. We don't want to make any new problems for you, but now we want to know how you finna resolve this issue that we have on our hands, being that you the one who fucked up our supply." Lockz loaded his 223 with a full clip and slide one inside the chamber.

"Nigga, fuck you! I don't owe you shit, buddy, and as far as my granddad, you gotta take that little loss and charge it to the game, my nigga."

By this time the whole team and Michael gathered around as Ghost spoke into the cellphone.

"You talk real greasy for a city slicking ass nigga over the phone, big man, but I think you might need to check your option list and let me run this shit by you again."

"The only thing you running to me is a dick sucker, potna. Now find you another line to try that slick ass game with."

"If you don't have those two hundred keys up here within the next three weeks, we gonna start mailing your bitch home piece by piece, nigga." Lockz then sparked up his blunt. "You might want to call your girl and check on her. She been gone to the store for a mighty long time."

"Call Erica," Ghost whispered to D-Lo as he held his hand over the phone.

"I'm sorry, did I hear you say something, or was that you apologizing for the way you just acted?" Lockz asked with authority.

As Ghost listened to Erica's phone ring, Lockz spoke through the phone. "A hold on my nigga. Let me handle this. Okay hello?" Lockz answered from Erica's phone and hung up his.

Ghost's heart dropped, already feeling the worst in his gut.

"Now, let's get back down to business."

"I'm listening," Ghost said, hoping that Erica was okay.

"Every few weeks that you don't send at least twenty-five percent of our shipment up here, I'm going to mail you a piece of her body. The situation that's at hand was your grandfather's problem, but being that you're the one who cancelled our connections, you're the one who has to make good and send the two hundred keys."

"What about the money? I can just pay you what the work is worth and you can let my bitch go, or I won't have any choice but to make my way up there if you force my hand." Ghost said, feeling that demon ready to creep to the surface.

"We don't want money, B. We want the chickens, and we don't want anything less than two hundred."

"Nigga, we gone get ya' little pussy ass money. You betta make sure my lady is left untouched, or you're gonna wish you never had anything to do with this situation." Ghost gritted his teeth, ready to psych out.

D-Lo, Michael, Tiffany, and Suave stood around as they listened to the up-north accent speak through the cell.

"Oh yeah, and one more thing, cuz," Lockz said with an evil tone.

"What?"

"Tell your dad that my boss said make sure he brings the fifty million dollars that he took from him a while back."

Michael listened to the New Yorker and knew exactly who he was referring to.

"If you ever want to see this bitch alive, gather that check, 'cause my people on the way." Lockz hung up the phone.

"Dad, what's going on? Who's their boss man, and who are these fucking people?" D-Lo asked, not believing what was going on.

Michael looked at his hands, sighing. "Were about to be at war with the Italians," he replied, looking at them all.

To Be Continued...
True Savage 3
Coming Soon

Stay Connected with Us!

Text **LOCKDOWN** to 22828 to stay up-to-date with new releases, sneak peaks, contests and more…

Thank you!

<u>Coming Soon from Lock Down Publications/Ca$h Presents</u>

BOW DOWN TO MY GANGSTA

By **Ca$h & Jamaica**

TORN BETWEEN TWO

By **Coffee**

BLOOD OF A BOSS **IV**

By **Askari**

BRIDE OF A HUSTLA **III**

THE FETTI GIRLS **III**

By **Destiny Skai**

WHEN A GOOD GIRL GOES BAD **II**

By **Adrienne**

LOVE & CHASIN' PAPER **II**

By **Qay Crockett**

THE HEART OF A GANGSTA **II**

By **Jerry Jackson**

TO DIE IN VAIN **II**

By **ASAD**

LOYAL TO THE GAME **IV**

By **TJ & Jelissa**

A DOPEBOY'S PRAYER **II**

By **Eddie "Wolf" Lee**

A HUSTLER'S DECEIT **III**

THE BOSS MAN'S DAUGHTERS **III**

BAE BELONGS TO ME **II**

By **Aryanna**

TRUE SAVAGE **III**

By **Chris Green**

RAISED AS A GOON **III**

By **Ghost**

IF LOVING YOU IS WRONG…

By **Jelissa**

BLOODY COMMAS

By **T.J.**

Available Now

(CLICK TO PURCHASE)

RESTRAINING ORDER **I & II**

By **CA$H & Coffee**

LOVE KNOWS NO BOUNDARIES **I II & III**

By **Coffee**

RAISED AS A GOON I & II

By **T.J.**

LAY IT DOWN **I & II**

LAST OF A DYING BREED

By **Jamaica**

LOYAL TO THE GAME

LOYAL TO THE GAME II

LOYAL TO THE GAME III

By **TJ & Jelissa**

PUSH IT TO THE LIMIT

By **Bre' Hayes**

BLOOD OF A BOSS **I II & III**

By **Askari**

THE STREETS BLEED MURDER **I, II & III**

THE HEART OF A GANGSTA

By **Jerry Jackson**

CUM FOR ME

CUM FOR ME 2

CUM FOR ME 3

An **LDP Erotica Collaboration**

BRIDE OF A HUSTLA **I & II**

THE FETTI GIRLS **I & II**

By **Destiny Skai**

WHEN A GOOD GIRL GOES BAD

By **Adrienne**

A GANGSTER'S REVENGE **I II III & IV**

THE BOSS MAN'S DAUGHTERS

THE BOSS MAN'S DAUGHTERS II

A SAVAGE LOVE **I & II**

BAE BELONGS TO ME

A HUSTLER'S DECEIT I, II

By **Aryanna**
A KINGPIN'S AMBITON
A KINGPIN'S AMBITION **II**

By **Ambitious**
TRUE SAVAGE

By **Chris Green**
A DOPEBOY'S PRAYER

By **Eddie "Wolf" Lee**
WHAT ABOUT US **I & II**
NEVER LOVE AGAIN
THUG ADDICTION

By **Kim Kaye**
THE KING CARTEL **I, II & III**

By **Frank Gresham**
THESE NIGGAS AIN'T LOYAL **I, II & III**

By **Nikki Tee**
GANGSTA SHYT **I II &III**

By **CATO**
THE ULTIMATE BETRAYAL

By **Phoenix**
BOSS'N UP **I & II**

By **Royal Nicole**
I LOVE YOU TO DEATH

By Destiny J

<u>I RIDE FOR MY HITTA</u>
<u>I STILL RIDE FOR MY HITTA</u>
By **Misty Holt**
<u>LOVE & CHASIN' PAPER</u>
By **Qay Crockett**
<u>TO DIE IN VAIN</u>
By **ASAD**

BOOKS BY LDP'S CEO, CA$H
(CLICK TO PURCHASE)

TRUST IN NO MAN

TRUST IN NO MAN 2

TRUST IN NO MAN 3

BONDED BY BLOOD

SHORTY GOT A THUG

THUGS CRY

THUGS CRY 2

THUGS CRY 3

TRUST NO BITCH

TRUST NO BITCH 2

TRUST NO BITCH 3

TIL MY CASKET DROPS

RESTRAINING ORDER

RESTRAINING ORDER 2

IN LOVE WITH A CONVICT

Coming Soon

BONDED BY BLOOD 2

BOW DOWN TO MY GANGSTA

True Savage 2

Made in the USA
Columbia, SC
10 August 2020